Little
Secrets

Over the Edge

Little
Sec

EMILY BLAKE

Over the Edge

Point

ISBN-13: 978-0-439-83681-4
ISBN-10: 0-439-83681-6

The text type was set in Utopia.
Book design by Steve Scott.

12 11 10 9 8 7 6 5 4 3 2 1   8 9 10 11 12 13/0

Printed in the U.S.A.   40

*For anyone standing near
the precipice . . .*

Chapter One

Tom Ramirez stared at the person behind the wheel of the silver Audi TT. He was finally looking into the face of his stalker — and he couldn't believe his eyes.

"Audra?" He blinked. It couldn't be. Except it was. His lab partner, Audra, the geeky class brain, was the person behind the insane number of notes and weird messages he'd been receiving. The person who'd been behind the tinted windows of the car that had been lurking nearby for weeks. Tom never would have guessed. Not in a million years. But here she was.

"Looking for a ride?" Audra asked casually.

As a matter of fact . . . Tom glanced over his shoulder at the Silver Spring Country Club, the sprawling white building he'd just stormed out of. He was supposed to be in there now, schmoozing and smiling, playing the good son. He would rather be somewhere else. Anywhere else. Tom's father, the district attorney, had just married the ultimate trophy bride in a disgusting display of pink and publicity, and the wedding reception was in full swing. If Tom left now, he was going to leave a gaping hole in Daddy Dearest's Congressional campaign photos. But Tom didn't care. At all. He was sick to death of doing what his father wanted. And he was about to stop. "Where are you going?" Tom asked.

"Anywhere you want." Audra looked at Tom, totally straight-faced.

That was all Tom needed to hear. Walking around to the passenger side of the car, he slid into the leather bucket seat. Before his door had even latched, the Audi was peeling out of the parking lot. Audra pointed the roadster out of town and floored it. Tom didn't look back.

"Looks like I showed up just in time," Audra

said after a few minutes of silence. "You came running out of the club pretty fast."

"What do you mean 'just in time'?" Tom shot back. "Weren't you out there waiting for me, the same way you've been waiting outside school, my house, the mall . . . the *bridal* shop? That was you following me, right?"

"Got me." Audra laughed sharply. Then in a lower tone she added, "I guess I've been waiting for you for a long time."

Tom looked at Audra carefully. Her chin-length dark hair was tucked behind her ears and her thin eyebrows curved into reclining question marks over the rimless glasses that shielded her dark brown eyes. She looked a little like a young Winona Ryder — with a geeky twist. For a brownnosing brainiac, she had a pretty hard edge. Tom had no idea what was up with her creepy stalker routine, but at that moment he didn't want to think about it. He was tired of thinking, and of pretending. Besides, Audra had just done him a huge favor: She'd helped him escape. He should really be grateful.

"Couldn't take it anymore, huh?" Audra asked, turning onto a wooded road.

Tom grimaced. *If you only knew*, he thought, flicking a shimmery pink flake of confetti from his tux.

"So what's the trouble?"

"Actually, if you really wanna know, it's everything," Tom blurted.

Audra kept her eyes on the curved road they were careening down and didn't say a word. She seemed to be waiting for Tom to say more, and he didn't disappoint.

"This whole stupid wedding . . ." Tom clenched his hands into fists. "It's so phony. I mean, it's not like my dad's in love with anything besides his own ambition. The only reason he's even marrying Deirdre is because he's going to run for Congress and wants us all to look like a happy family. Which, believe me, we are not," he added to remove all doubt.

Audra nodded, but she didn't ask questions or try to reassure him that it wasn't as bad as he thought. She just listened. And it felt so good to let it all out that Tom went on.

"And it's been even worse since Zoey got back. She totally sets Dad off, and then he zeroes in on me. It's like boarding school turned her

4

into some kind of psycho pyro or something. She's totally different now."

Audra's right eyebrow shot up at the mention of Tom's twin sister, but she still didn't comment. Tom was vaguely aware that Audra and Zoey had their own beef. They had been at odds for a while now, ever since Zoey started doing well in school. Apparently she was threatening Audra's status as top brain or something. Tom realized he probably shouldn't be trashing Zoey in front of Audra. For a second he almost wished he cared.

"It's embarrassing, you know? Being related to a freak. Not that I care what anyone thinks, but . . ." Tom ran a hand through his thick dark hair, grabbing a handful and hanging on. "We *used* to be friends, but not anymore. Not that my 'real' friends are any better. Chad is so ga-ga over Kelly that he couldn't care less about his supposed best friend . . . oh, unless he needs help with his schoolwork. I guess playing boyfriend takes up too much time for him to think about anything other than Kelly. And then I have to bail him out almost every day. Like I have nothing better to do than *his* homework."

"Yeah, that Kelly is something else." Audra wrinkled her nose, not bothering to hide her disdain for Kelly Reeves, the reigning queen of Stafford Academy, the private prep school where they were all sophomores. "I can't believe what guys do for her."

Tom flinched. Audra's words were all too true. If Kelly would only let him, he would do anything for her . . . his best friend's girlfriend. Anything. Tom had been in love with Kelly since elementary school. She was supposed to be with him, not with Chad. And what did Tom do about it? Chad's homework!

Still, who was Audra — a lunatic stalker — to judge Kelly Reeves? Tom couldn't believe he'd just totally spilled his guts to his wacko lab partner. He'd better watch it or he'd reveal too much — like how he really felt about Kelly.

"Everyone's just making me crazy right now." Tom let his seat belt pull him back in his seat. He hadn't realized how hard he had been straining against it. As the belt went slack, Tom felt some of the tension within him slacken, too. The horrible compressed feeling that had been building in his chest for weeks was subsiding as he unloaded his gripes. And it felt good.

Without saying a word, Audra looked over at Tom, nodded once, and gave him a tight, knowing smile. It was just a tiny sign that she'd heard him, but for some weird reason it made Tom's throat clench. He couldn't remember the last time somebody had asked him what was wrong and actually listened to his answer.

He felt a hundred times better, and he hadn't even told Audra about what was *really* bothering him, about the horrible secret he had suspected for weeks, but had only just confirmed. Right before he'd run out of the wedding reception, Tom had basically accused his father of having murdered his and Zoey's mother . . . and his father hadn't denied it. Tom clenched his jaw in renewed frustration. Even now that he knew the truth, there was nothing he could do about it. His mother's death had long ago been declared an accident.

Almost on cue, Audra swerved into a gravel pullout next to a lake, and Tom shuddered. Until that moment, he hadn't even noticed where they'd been headed. He had been avoiding this place for years. It was the lake at Great Falls, the lake his mother had drowned in. Not the exact spot, but still.

Tom sat there, barely breathing. Did Audra know?

"I want to show you something." Audra got out of the car and walked around to Tom's side. She opened his door and pulled his hand. "Come on." She smiled.

She couldn't know. It's just a freaky coincidence, Tom told himself. As if in a trance, he got out and followed Audra down a narrow path that ran along the lake. The autumn air chilled him through the jacket of his tuxedo, and his ridiculous wedding shoes slid on the rocky trail. He wasn't exactly dressed for hiking.

Sensing his reluctance, Audra paused and looked over her shoulder. "It's worth it. I promise," she assured him.

For some reason Tom believed her. He breathed in the bracing wind and shivered. The relief he had been feeling before they got to the lake began to return. Maybe this was what he needed — to stop living a charade and face things head-on.

The two walked in silence as the trail sloped up. Audra was clearly familiar with the path, but she slowed her pace so Tom could keep up in his treadless shoes. They continued climbing until Tom was nearly out of breath. Pausing, he looked down. They were at least fifteen feet above the lake and the view was great. The fall leaves were just starting to turn. Ahead, Tom could hear the sound of running water.

"Almost there," Audra announced. "Just around the bend." When they rounded the corner, Tom stopped on a rocky outcropping to take in the incredible view. Before them was a waterfall crashing into deep water below. When he turned he could see the town of Silver Spring behind them.

The sound of the pounding water became the only sound in Tom's head. His mind was clear for the first time in what felt like forever. Audra was right. It was worth it.

Tom stood in place as the dark-haired girl scooted closer and closer to the edge of the cliff and peered over the side. She stared into the water for a long moment, looking mesmerized. Then she looked back at Tom. "Wanna jump?" she asked mischievously.

Tom laughed, but a second later Audra removed her glasses and he realized that she was not joking. The laugh died in his throat. "You're serious?" he asked.

"As cancer," she replied, kicking off her shoes.

"Wait —" Tom reached out to stop her, but Audra took two steps and was gone. For an eerie moment there was no noise but the crashing falls. Then a splash.

Tom's chest tightened. He rushed to the edge and looked over, afraid of what he might see.

Far below Audra bobbed to the surface, looked up, and laughed. "Come on!" she called, beckoning. "Jump."

Tom hesitated. What was he afraid of? What was he hanging on for? It was time to let go. Backing up a few steps, Tom ran. He launched himself off the edge of the rock. The next thing he knew, he was flying through the air toward the churning water below.

Chapter Two

Alison Rose sat on the floor of her father's home office, staring at his empty desk, the empty shelves . . . the emptiness. Except for a few pieces of large furniture and the small silver key she held in her hand, everything in the house she had lived in for the past fifteen years — her whole life — was gone. And so was her dad.

Rolling back, Alison lay flat on the floor and stared at the ceiling. Her dad had vanished. Her mom was in jail awaiting trial for embezzlement, grand larceny, and tax fraud. And her grand-mother . . . oh, if only she would disappear, too. Alison could not remember ever feeling as alone as she did right then.

Alison let out a scream into the abandoned mansion. Her frustration echoed off the vaulted ceiling, mocking her. Maybe she should have listened to her father's warning the last time they spoke. Maybe she should have come looking for him sooner. But she had been living in luxury's lap at Grandmother Diamond's estate for the past few weeks, and she'd had no idea that her father was about to disappear to who-knows-where.

Slowly, the emptiness inside of Alison was replaced by fury. *Why am I blaming myself for this*? she wondered. He's *the one who abandoned* me. Anger bubbled up, threatening to erupt. Maybe if her dad hadn't been falling apart so badly, drinking himself into a stupor, she wouldn't have had to snap on the "Diamond" leash and collar and move in with her controlling, manipulative grandmother in the first place. Her dad couldn't pull it together enough to take care of his own daughter, but he could pull it together enough to pack up the entire mansion and leave? Without telling her where he was going? It was too much.

And, Alison realized, it just didn't make sense.

With a shudder, Alison recognized how incredibly unlikely it was that her father could have pulled off leaving town on his own. The man couldn't manage to return a phone call. And with all of the Rose family assets frozen following Alison's mother's arrest, he had no money. No way could he get rid of all their possessions, pack a bag, get a flight, and go. Alison's blood ran cold as the pieces came together in her head. Somebody had helped Jack Rose disappear, or worse, *made* him disappear. Somebody wanted him out of the picture and the Rose family completely dismantled — somebody who always got her way.

Alison seethed. She knew exactly who was cunning enough, callous enough, and powerful enough to pull off such a scheme: her grandmother, Tamara Diamond. The woman was behind *everything*. Wielding her wealth like a weapon, she ruled the entire town — and her own family. It was because of Grandmother Diamond that Alison's mother, Helen, was in jail. It was Grandmother Diamond who'd had the room Alison was living in at the Diamond estate ransacked earlier that day. She had done it to make sure Alison wasn't planning to double-cross her, to make sure Alison knew whose thumb she was really under. Grandmother Diamond had wanted to make clear to Alison how easily she could destroy her if Alison came forward with the papers she had stolen from her grandmother's secret vault — the papers that proved Tamara's involvement in Alison's mother's arrest. And now, somehow, Tamara had managed to get rid of Jack. But why? *To hurt me*, Alison thought. *To take away the one person who might actually be on my side. To force me to rely on her completely.*

Alison's anger began to turn to despair. *If only I had realized* . . . she thought miserably. *If only I had realized* . . . *Then what?* Then probably nothing. She was powerless, especially where her grandmother was concerned.

Until recently, Grandmother Diamond had been Alison's most powerful ally. Alison had always been her grandmother's favorite, in spite of a long-standing feud between Tamara and Alison's mother, Helen. Being in Tamara's good graces had some definite benefits — starting with how much their closeness annoyed Alison's mother. Then Helen had been arrested — and it certainly looked as though Alison's grandmother was responsible. Left with no choice but to try and uncover the truth, Alison had stolen some papers from her grandmother's secret vault. And somehow her grandmother knew she'd done it because since then her room had been ransacked and her father had disappeared.

A sob of frustration was growing in Alison's throat. Grandmother Diamond controlled *everything*. She was as ruthless as she was wealthy, and since everyone in Silver Spring was under her power, there was nowhere to turn. For the first time, Alison realized what a dangerous enemy Tamara Diamond could be to her personally. The ransacked room was a warning — her father's disappearance, a threat. And as sick as she was of being controlled, Alison knew she had no choice but to go back to Tamara's mansion and continue playing the game — by her grandmother's rules. Maybe if Alison just played along, it wouldn't be so bad. Maybe if she returned to her grandmother's team now, Tamara might not hold a grudge. Alison knew that when she *did* play by the rules, under her grandmother's wing was the safest place to be. Tamara took good care of those that took care of her. On more than one occasion Grandmother Diamond had pulled Alison's backstabbing cousin Kelly's claws out of her skin. And once she'd even shown Alison she had a softer side, crying about her estranged relationship with Alison's mom. Yes, Alison would go back.

"But not right now," she whispered into the empty house. She needed something, if only a little time, for herself.

Looking down at her hands, Alison realized she had been clenching them in tight fists. Slowly she uncurled her fingers to stare at the little silver key that lay in her right palm. Her father had left the key wrapped in a piece of blank paper in an envelope with her name on it. There were no instructions. No note. Nothing to say where he had gone, why he had left, or what the key might open. Alison would have to figure all of that out on her own.

Chapter Three

Starting in the den, Alison walked through the now-empty mansion that used to be her home, trying the key in every lock she could find, even though it was clearly too small to unlock most of them. She moved from the office to the living room, the dining room, the kitchen, the butler's pantry, the laundry room, and the front hall. From there she scoured the servants' quarters, the game room, the gym, the home theater, her mother's office, and the library. After she'd finished the first floor she headed upstairs to check the bedrooms, stopping just outside her old room. The door was partially closed, and she pushed it lightly, letting it swing open.

Alison gasped. She'd known her room would be as empty as the rest of the house, but actually seeing it was still a blow. Her bed, her stereo, her books and clothes and trinkets were gone. It was as if her old life had been erased and no longer existed.

And the truth was, it didn't. Everything had changed since the night her mother had been arrested. Her best friend and cousin, Kelly, had turned on her, stealing her boyfriend Chad, who publicly humiliated her by dumping her in front of half the school. As if it wasn't already humiliating enough that photos of her mother the prisoner were splashed across the front page of every newspaper and tabloid and featured on every news show. If it hadn't been for Grandmother Diamond's favor — and the reappearance of her best friend, Zoey — Alison might not have made it through that time.

Quickly Alison reached for the knob and closed the door to her room. There was no use pining for the past.

After a thorough search of her parents' room, the guest rooms, and the upstairs den, Alison had exhausted all the possibilities — and was exhausted herself.

Frustrated, sad, and tired, Alison threw herself down on the floor in the living room beside the bags she'd hurriedly packed when she'd fled her grandmother's and stared up at the frescoed ceiling. She was stalling now. Zoey's dad's wedding reception would be over soon, and her grandmother would expect Alison to be at the Diamond estate when she arrived home.

The thought of returning to Tamara's brought tears to Alison's eyes. She was not a guest in her grandmother's house. She was a prisoner, just like her mother. The only real difference was that Alison's cell was padded in wealth and the bars on her cage were twenty-four-karat gold.

Alison was not ready for lockdown. Not yet. Picking up her phone, she made a quick call.

"Hi, Louise." She was relieved when the housekeeper picked up. Tamara Diamond almost never answered her own phone, of course, and she was probably still at the Ramirez wedding reception, but you never knew when she would surprise you. And it was much easier to lie to the help than to Her Highness.

"Can you please tell Grandmother that I'm staying at Zoey's tonight? I'll be home in the morning," she said. She snapped the phone shut quickly. There. It was done.

Pulling her Moschino trench coat from one of her suitcases, Alison curled up on the floor. She closed her eyes and tried to shut out the events of the past day — of the past week — of the past few months. She tried hard to remember back to a time when things were good, when she was happy. It was not easy.

She was just drifting off to sleep when there was a loud knock on the door.

Chapter Four

Zoey yanked the poufy pink monstrosity of a bridesmaid's gown over her head and threw it on her bedroom floor. "Take that," she said, stomping on it. She had never been so happy to remove a piece of clothing in her life. The wedding was over. The pink stretch Hummer had sailed, and DA Daddy and his icky new wife were off on their honeymoon for two whole weeks.

If only they were going to be gone longer, Zoey thought as she pulled on a pair of well-worn jeans and her Kings of Leon concert T-shirt. Back in her old skin, Zoey took one more kick at the dress, and headed downstairs to get something to drink. Fake-smiling all day for the guests and

cameras and pulling double duty for her disappearing brother was irritating, thirsty work.
She was looking forward to taking a load off
and doing some serious vegetating in front of
the TV.

Crushed ice dropped into Zoey's glass from
the refrigerator door. Waiting for it to fill, Zoey
looked absently out the tall windows that framed
the front door. A car was pulling into the drive, a
silver Audi with a stupid-looking clown head on
the antenna. Wasn't that Audra's car? What was
Audra Wilson doing here?

*If that evil nutcase thinks she can harass me
about academics in my own home, she'd best
think again.* Zoey stopped filling her glass and
walked toward the entry hall, ready for a confrontation. What she saw made her jaw drop.

It was not Audra who climbed out — though
it was certainly her car. It was Tom! Zoey stood
stock-still, unable to move, unable to close her
gaping mouth as her brother unfolded himself
from the passenger seat and walked in the
door carrying his sopping pink tie and cummer-
bund. He was soaking wet from top to tail. He

looked like a shivering, near-drowned penguin. And he had no shoes. Weirder still, he was smiling — something Zoey hadn't seen her twin do in weeks.

Quickly coming to her senses, Zoey walked back to the kitchen and filled her glass with iced tea from the fridge. "'Sup?" she said, trying to sound casual. Tom, who had hardly been friendly since Zoey had returned to Silver Spring after getting kicked out of her fifth boarding school in a row, had been especially on edge lately — a razor's edge. If she wanted to get any information out of him about the big blowup she had seen between him and their father — or why Audra Wilson had dropped him off at home all wet — she knew she had to play it cool.

"Out for a little swim?" she asked, keeping her voice breezy. "Audra giving you lessons? I hear she's pretty smart."

Tom stared at her like she was something gross he had just stepped in. "What do you care?" he growled. "You're not my mother. She's dead, remember?"

Zoey staggered back like Tom had slapped

her. *Whoa.* She raised a hand in surrender. How could he even say that? They had *both* lost their mother, and there wasn't a day or even a minute during which either of them forgot that. Zoey looked at Tom cautiously. "Geez. Sorry." She reached a hand out toward her brother in truce. "I didn't realize —"

Tom slapped Zoey's hand away. "No. You never realize, Zoey. So don't touch me. In fact, don't even look at me. And stop acting like you can just waltz back in here after five years and pick up where we left off. I don't need you anymore." Tom's voice was strained and his hands were trembling. "I don't need anyone," he snarled before stomping up the stairs and slamming the bathroom door.

"Clearly," Zoey said under her breath when he was gone. Tom's outburst left Zoey feeling shaken. She knew Tom had been bottling a lot of stuff up, but she hadn't been expecting him to take it out on her. *Stupid me for thinking we could be friends.*

Feeling gloomy, Zoey walked up to her room and softly closed the door. She turned on the TV for some noise and company but didn't have a long enough attention span to watch even a commercial.

What was up with her brother? And what in the world was he doing hanging out with Audra? Zoey was the first person to admit Tom needed some new friends. Kelly and Chad were as plastic as Barbie and Ken, and about as deep. But Audra? She was kinda . . . crazy. The girl had it in for Zoey for the simple reason that she had started doing well in school. Audra had actually threatened Zoey over her grades. That was more than just competitive. It was ridiculous.

Zoey took a huge swig of her iced tea. "Oh." The cold liquid went right to her head. She squeezed one eye shut. Brain freeze.

She needed someone to vent to. She needed to call Alison. When her head had thawed, Zoey grabbed her phone off the dresser. She dialed Alison's cell number and held the phone to her ear. No answer.

Hitting the END button, Zoey flopped back on her bed. Great. Alison was MIA. Now she was worried about two people: her brother and her best friend.

Alison had to have been feeling pretty cruddy

to leave the reception early — she wouldn't have abandoned Zoey if she'd just had a slight headache. She knew how much Zoey had been dreading the event. It was a big deal to bag. And now she wasn't picking up. Where was that girl?

Chapter Five

Alison's eyes flew open. No, she hadn't dreamed it. There really was someone knocking. *Dad?* She threw off the trench coat and stumbled toward the entry hall. Back in the living room her cell phone began to ring, but she ignored it. The pounding on the door sounded much more insistent.

Putting her eye to the peephole, Alison peered out. The guy on the doorstep wasn't her dad. It was Jeremy, Zoey's tutor. Weird. After glancing in the huge entry mirror and doing what she could with her hair, she unlocked the door.

"Hey." Alison greeted Jeremy casually. Jeremy's mouth dropped open. He looked almost as surprised to see her as she was to see him. Except that this was *her* house. She tried to think of how to ask him what he was doing there without sounding rude.

"Oh, hey. I was just passing through the neighborhood and thought I'd stop by," Jeremy said kind of lamely. "See how you were doing."

Alison squinted at his handsome, stubbled face. Didn't he know she was staying with her grandmother these days?

"Is, uh, your dad here?" Jeremy looked past Alison into the empty house.

"No. Just me," Alison said. For a brief second she wondered if she should close the door in Jeremy's face. What was he doing here asking about her dad? She didn't actually know him well enough to rule out the possibility of him being some kind of creep. But she didn't feel like she was in danger, and she knew Zoey trusted him. They spent a lot of time together. Besides, it felt kind of nice to have company, any company. "Wanna come in?" She held the door open and Jeremy stepped inside a little gingerly.

"Sure." Standing in the front hall, he shifted his weight from one foot to the other and looked into Alison's face. "Um, are you okay?" he asked gently, raising his eyebrows.

Alison forced a smile. She must have looked as spooked as she felt. "I've been better," she said honestly. Zoey had told her that Jeremy had a way of making you spill your guts, and she was right. Maybe it was the dimples.

Luckily Jeremy let the subject drop. He stood awkwardly in the entryway, shoving his hands deeper into his pockets and glancing toward the other rooms. "Wow. Your house looks totally cleared out."

Alison nodded but didn't offer an explanation.

"You want a tour anyway?" Alison asked. He seemed curious. And even though it had been almost completely cleaned out, Helen Rose's house was still a sight to behold. A household name, Alison's mother had written the book on style: *Helen Rose's Looking Good*. She had her own magazine as well as an extensive line of household items. The Rose family home had been designed by Helen's own team of architects. She oversaw every detail and it was regularly featured in her magazine.

"Sure!" Jeremy's face lit up. "I mean, if you don't mind."

Yep. True sign of a fan. Alison wondered if Jeremy was one of those college kids who dreamed of working for Helen Rose one day. To Alison that sounded like a nightmare — but that was because she knew the boss, and all too well.

Alison led Jeremy from room to room, retracing the steps she had taken looking for the lock to her mystery key. But with Jeremy in tow she could look at the house in a new light. He appreciated all of her mom's little design details. It almost made Alison feel proud, an emotion she hadn't associated with her family — especially her mom — in a long time.

"Is this real?" Jeremy reached down to touch a delicate gold inlay pattern on the floor between the living and dining rooms.

"Of course." Alison laughed. "Helen Rose does not do fake — unless you consider the accounts." *And her family*, she thought.

"That has yet to be proven," Jeremy said solemnly.

Wait. Was Jeremy sticking up for her mom? Alison looked at him. He looked totally earnest.

Rabid fan, she decided. And the funny thing was, she didn't think less of him for it. Zoey was right about him. He was easy to like and easy to talk to. There was something kind in his eyes. And it didn't hurt that he was certifiably adorable.

"You don't really think your mom is guilty, do you?" Jeremy pressed.

Alison stood silent, stunned by the directness of his question. *Do I think she's guilty?* she asked herself. Honestly, she was not sure. The only thing she was certain of was that she held only a few pieces of this complicated puzzle — and that she needed to find out the whole story. "No," she said to Jeremy, a little feebly, wishing she really meant it. She wanted to believe that her mom was innocent, but she could not ignore the nagging feeling in her gut that told her different.

"Well, thanks for the tour." Jeremy dropped the uncomfortable topic and shoved his hands into his jacket pockets. "I guess I should go, but . . ." He paused. The silence was weird.

Alison wished he weren't leaving but didn't think it would be a good idea to ask him to stay. She opened the door.

"Is there anything I can do for you?" Jeremy asked.

Alison spotted Jeremy's car in the driveway, a sporty little black Saab. She looked back into the living room, where she had hauled the pile of luggage she'd brought over in a cab. "Actually," she said, getting an idea, "there is. Would you mind giving me a ride to Zoey's?"

Chapter Six

Zoey glanced at the clock. The shower was still running. Tom had disappeared into the bathroom over an hour ago and still hadn't emerged. When he did he would probably look like a raisin. She hoped he hadn't slipped and hit his head or anything. Or maybe that would be a good thing. It might actually help him shake his lousy mood.

If he's not out in half an hour, I'm calling 911, she thought grimly. She wouldn't really. EMTs busting in on her twin in the tub would do nothing to improve their strained relationship.

Downstairs the door chime sounded and Zoey pushed her concerns about her brother aside. She padded barefoot into the front hall to see who it was, guessing that it would be the caterers bringing the leftover food from the reception. And just in time. Zoey had finally gotten her appetite back after the nauseating matrimonial display.

What she found on the front porch made her stomach flip again. "Jeremy? Alison?" she said as she opened the door. *Together? With luggage?*

"Zoey!" Alison dropped her heavy bags on the floor and gave Zoey a tight hug. "Do you mind if I spend the night?"

Zoey shrugged and grinned. "Of course not." But she was still baffled. Why had her best friend turned up with her crush? She looked from Alison to Jeremy and back. She wasn't jealous, exactly. It was just weird. Alison met her gaze and raised her eyebrows — she looked like she knew what Zoey was asking, and she had a lot to say, only not in front of the guy standing behind her. Zoey would have to get the whole story later.

Sensing the need for an explanation, Jeremy spoke up. "Alison needed a ride, so I thought I would try my hand at chauffeuring," he joked.

"You're doing so well with your schoolwork now, I think my days as a tutor might be numbered." Jeremy grinned.

Zoey grimaced. "Yeah, right."

"I don't know." Alison laughed and took her other bags from Jeremy. "Your driving days may be limited, too. I think chauffeurs are supposed to carry *all* the bags."

Zoey eyed the car in the driveway. "And isn't your ride a little small to belong to a hired driver — and a little *nice* to belong to a tutor?" Zoey asked, jumping at the chance to tease Jeremy.

Jeremy turned back to look at the new black two-door Saab parked in the drive. He blushed. Zoey guessed the car had been a real splurge. She had seen it before and he seemed really proud of it.

"Sweet, huh? I got it for graduation," Jeremy explained, looking at his keys. "Little gift from my mom. Making up for the last eighteen years, I guess."

Alison nodded like she knew exactly what he was talking about. She was a girl who often got gifts in lieu of time, love, or company. Zoey got expensive schools and tutors, and a lot of lectures.

"Anyway . . ." Jeremy held up his hand casually. "I'll work on the finer details of my new profession and get back to you." He nodded to Alison and tipped an invisible hat. "I can only aspire to work for a family as prestigious as the Roses."

Zoey rolled her eyes. Jeremy was laying it on a little thick. As far as she was concerned, his obsession with the Roses was his biggest flaw.

Even Alison looked a little taken aback as she thanked him for the ride.

"Yeah," Zoey echoed. "Thanks for dropping her off." Normally Zoey would have asked Jeremy to come in and hang out. She liked to stretch out her time with him for as long as possible. But right now she wanted Alison alone. She could tell Alison was anxious to talk to her, too.

When Jeremy was finally gone, Zoey helped Alison lug her bags into the living room. "How's your head?" she asked, sitting cross-legged on the couch.

For a second Alison looked confused. She touched her forehead. "Oh. My head. Geez. I'm so sorry I had to leave the reception, Zo. Was that today? So much has happened, it feels like your dad's wedding was a million years ago."

"So, let's have it." Zoey patted the spot next to her on the couch.

Alison sat down beside Zoey. She pulled her knees up and rested her chin on them. She took a deep breath. Then she let loose.

Zoey's eyes opened wider and wider as Alison filled her in on her ransacked room, her decision to leave her grandmother's house, and her dad's disappearance. "He didn't even leave a note," she said, her eyes filling up with tears. "Just this stupid little key."

"Oh, Alison." Zoey grabbed a tissue and passed it over before wrapping her arms around her friend for a quick hug. Alison had been through a *lot* since her mother's arrest, but this was the first time Zoey had seen her cry. "You think your grandmother is behind it?"

Alison sniffled. "I don't even know what to think," she said. "But that's my best guess."

Zoey's eyes flashed with anger on Alison's behalf. "Then you have to confront her. What have you got to lose?"

Alison gulped and nodded. "I thought you might say that. And I know that you're right. But I've got nowhere else to go. She's the one paying my tuition. And . . ." Alison broke off. She looked into Zoey's face. "I wish I didn't have to go back there, ever." She smiled weakly. "Maybe your dad and Deirdre would like to adopt me."

"Ugh." Zoey grimaced. "Be careful what you wish for." But she was glad to hear Alison making a joke.

"At least you can stay here tonight," Zoey added. "We'll deal with tomorrow when we get there." She grabbed another tissue and forced herself to smile as she handed it over. "Besides, your grandmother hasn't won yet. Your mom still gets a trial. And we've still got the documents," she added, thinking of the manila envelope stuffed under her mattress.

Alison shook her head. "I don't even care which of them wins anymore. I'm just sick of being caught in the middle."

Zoey squeezed her friend's hand.

Now was definitely not the time to ask Alison about how Jeremy fit into the story. It was probably nothing. Besides, Alison had more than enough to deal with already.

Chapter Seven

"Thank you, Grandmother," Kelly said, taking a gold-rimmed teacup and saucer from Tamara Diamond's jewel-adorned hands. "I just needed someone to talk to, someone who would understand." She paused and took a sip of hot tea. Ugh. Unsweetened. "It's all been pretty overwhelming!" she added with the sigh of someone who was emotionally overwrought but bravely holding it together. Might as well play her situation for all it was worth. A good enough reason to "seek comfort" from Grandmother Diamond didn't come around very often.

When Aunt Christine had first told Kelly that she was her real mother, Kelly had been stunned.

It had never even *occurred* to her that Phoebe, the mother who raised her, might not have given birth to her. But in a way it made sense. Phoebe had always been a little . . . dull. Kelly had so much more in common with her actress "aunt"— love of attention, dramatic prowess, fierce good looks. Kelly's cutting-edge, trail-blazing style had never been in step with Phoebe's milquetoast sensibilities. Unfortunately, Aunt Christine had made it all too clear that she still had no interest in playing mom. Christine had never wanted Kelly as a daughter, not then and not now. And that hurt. So Kelly did what she did with any pain. She buried it deep inside, where she could dig it out only when it would serve her well. Like now.

Grandmother Diamond reached out and patted Kelly's hand as if she were a cactus. "Of course it's overwhelming, my dear," she said in her clipped way. "I'm surprised you didn't come to me sooner."

Kelly tucked a lock of blond hair behind an ear and blinked back nonexistent tears. "I didn't want to upset you," she explained. "You've had so much to deal with already, with the burden of taking care of Alison while Aunt Helen is in jail." She emphasized the word *burden* just so. It was a cheap shot at her best-friend-turned-worst-enemy, but Kelly knew that their grandmother appreciated the rivalry — and knocking Alison down a notch in their grandmother's esteem was half the point of Kelly's late-morning visit. "And of course you already knew that Aunt Christine is my real mother. But when she told me, that night of the fire . . . and then left town the next day as if nothing had happened, well . . ." She trailed off, covering her face with her hands. "I felt like I'd lost two mothers at once. It was terrible — worse than having a mother in jail!"

Tamara smirked and let a little puff of air out her nose, acknowledging Kelly's dig at her cousin's expense. Kelly savored her grandmother's approval. Tamara Diamond was a master of manipulation. It was a true pleasure to play this game with her . . . especially since Kelly usually felt like she was playing *against* her.

Clearing her throat, Grandmother Diamond signaled she was about to change gears and expected Kelly's full attention. Kelly tried not to look bored and hoped the lecture would be short. "You listen to me, Kelly Diamond Reeves. Phoebe is a much better mother than Christine could ever be. You're lucky to have been raised by her. I think you know that."

Kelly nodded serenely, as if she were paying close attention to every word.

"Of course it was a shock for you to hear the truth — and frankly, I am not pleased that Christine told you without asking my permission first. It was poor judgment on her part, to say the least. But the important thing to remember is that you're a Diamond, and no one can deny you your heritage. Nothing can ever take that sparkle — or those essential hard edges — away." Tamara's eyes gleamed and she raised her chin slightly. "This silly little secret changes nothing."

Kelly tossed her hair back with exhilaration. As far as Grandmother Diamond's little lessons went, that wasn't a bad one — not at all. And she couldn't remember the last time she and her grandmother had talked like this, the last time Her Highness had spoken approvingly of Kelly. It was almost like they were allies. Almost.

"Don't play with your hair, Kelly,"

Grandmother Diamond snapped. "It's self-indulgent."

Kelly resisted the urge to get to her feet in a huff. That last crack coming from the most self-serving woman in the world was laughable. Who was Tamara kidding? But Kelly couldn't roll her eyes or even just ignore the comment as she would have done a week ago. She had to act like she took every bit of criticism to heart, like she actually cared what her grandmother thought. Because up to that minute, this little get-together had been going swimmingly. And Kelly needed that — needed to keep her relationship with her grandmother on a more positive track. Never peachy, things between them had taken a turn for the worse when Kelly had staged a surprise attack on Tamara's favorite grand-daughter, Alison. In one fell swoop, Kelly had stolen Alison's boyfriend and humiliated her in front of all of Stafford Academy, knocking her into a social no-man's-land right when Alison was at her most vulnerable — just after Helen Rose had been arrested. Kelly had never imag-ined her grandmother would not approve of her victory. After all, she'd learned nearly all of her underhanded tactics from observing the old woman. And, if Aunt Christine's hunch was correct, Tamara herself had framed Alison's mother in the first place. But instead of celebrating Kelly, Grandmother Diamond had taken perfect little Alison under her wing like a mother hen. It was enough to make Kelly seriously sick. But Kelly couldn't afford to let Alison keep Grandmother Diamond on her side, so she'd come here to grovel.

"You are right, of course," Kelly agreed, straightening her shoulders like her grandmother had been telling her to do since she was three. "About everything," she added, just in case it wasn't obvious. She picked up her teacup and saucer and managed to get a dainty sip down without gagging. She hated unsweetened tea almost as much as she hated Alison. But Grandmother Diamond scoffed at people who added sugar.

Kelly set her teacup down. She was about to elaborate on the topic she and her grandmother were enjoying most — how Alison was such a difficult cross for her grandmother to bear — when she saw someone step into the room.

Looking toward the parlor door, she smiled wickedly and folded her hands in her lap. Alison, the about-to-be-dethroned family favorite, had finally arrived. She was standing in the doorway looking like a deer in the headlights — surprised and immobile. Typical.

Kelly inched a bit closer to her grandmother just to make sure Alison picked up on her new family position. The girl could be a little slow. "Oh, Alison," she said with a sweet smile. "Were your ears burning? We were just talking about you." She picked up her teacup and raised it as if in a toast. "Care for a cup of tea?" she offered.

Chapter Eight

Alison stood in the doorway staring stupidly at the scene in front of her. She couldn't help it. It was just so surprising and infuriating. Not to mention more than a little scary. Just when her beyond-evil cousin and ex-best friend was finally backing off at school, it appeared that she'd decided to come torture Alison at Grandmother Diamond's estate — a place Kelly normally avoided like the plague. And Alison was certain that this was no casual visit. This was a new scheme. Apparently, having the upper hand at Stafford Academy was not enough. Kelly was out to conquer the home turf, too.

Alison gazed at Kelly, who was practically

snuggled up to their grandmother on the elegant sofa. It was not a cozy scene. What were these two up to?

Nothing you can't dismantle, she told herself as she braced for the worst. Because ever since Alison and Kelly were little girls, one thing had been clear: Alison was her grandmother's favorite. Even the twists and turns of the last few weeks — and of the last twenty-four hours — hadn't changed that. And if Kelly thought she could just waltz in and wrap Tamara around her little finger while Alison sat there and watched, she had another thing coming. So what if Tamara had framed Alison's mother and masterminded her father's disappearance? So what if just yesterday Alison had wanted to gnaw through the tether her grandmother kept her on? Being Grandmother Diamond's favorite was still the one thing Alison had over Kelly. Whether it was a real choice or not, it guaranteed her protection, and put her in a fantastic position to be wealthy for the rest of her life. Though nobody in the family, save Her Highness, had ever seen "the list," Alison felt sure her name ranked over Kelly's in their grandmother's will, and she wanted to keep it that way. No way was she going to let it go without a fight.

"I'd love some tea," Alison purred sweetly as she crossed the room and sat down on the other side of Grandmother Diamond. She poured herself a cup and coolly took a sip. "Don't you take sugar with yours, Kelly?" Alison asked, knowing full well their grandmother's opinion on sweeteners. "I'm sure Francesca didn't even think to bring out a sugar bowl, since she knows I outgrew using it years ago. Here, I'll call her." She reached for the bell that summoned the help, but Kelly reached out and stopped her.

"Really, Alison," Kelly said with a fake smile, "no need to play hostess. You're just as much of a guest here as I am."

Alison laughed easily. "If you say so," she said. "I didn't realize you were so touchy about it." She turned to Tamara and spoke with exaggerated sympathy. "I'm sorry, Grandmother. I hope you haven't had to put up with Kelly's dramatics all morning. I know firsthand how tedious that can be. But then, I suppose we must indulge her, since she's family." She sighed and sat back with her cup.

Kelly was silent as she glared at her cousin. It took her a full five seconds to come up with something to say, an unusually long time for her, Alison noted with pride. Kelly must not have been expecting Alison to open on the offensive. Her battle skills were obviously up to snuff, in spite of, or maybe because of, everything she'd been through lately.

"How's Aunt Helen? How long has it been since you visited your jailbird mother, Alison?" Kelly asked. "I noticed she's on the front cover of all the tabloids again this week."

Alison saw a tiny smile on Tamara's face as Alison turned to face Kelly more fully. The matriarch was enjoying this. "I can't recall when I saw her last," Alison replied with a shrug. "But are you sure you want to talk about mothers, Kelly? I would imagine it's a sensitive subject for you, since you just learned yours didn't want you — then or now."

Kelly flinched, Grandmother Diamond smirked, and Alison felt a thrill of victory. But as she gazed at her cousin's cold face she suddenly felt guilty. That had been a low blow, and it didn't feel good to fight down on Kelly's level.

Even though she knew she had gone too far, there was no way Alison was going to apologize. Kelly didn't deserve it, and Grandmother Diamond would probably take it as a sign of Alison's weakness. So instead, she pushed it one step further. "Oops — did I forget to mention that I knew about that little secret?" Alison had been listening in the hall when Aunt Christine had spilled the beans.

Kelly was still blinking back her surprise when Grandmother Diamond set her teacup down and cleared her throat.

"That will be all, Kelly," she announced, as if they'd come to the end of a business meeting. "Thank you so much for coming."

Kelly's expression shifted into one of annoyance. She hated being dismissed, and both Alison and Tamara knew it. "Kelly," Grandmother Diamond repeated sternly when the girl didn't get immediately to her feet. "We'll see you next Sunday."

Alison savored the moment. It was not a large

victory, but it was a sweet one. She had come back to Grandmother Diamond's house just in time, and it felt good to reaffirm their alliance right under Kelly's perky nose.

Setting her teacup and saucer down with a clatter, Kelly stood up. "I was actually just about to excuse myself, Grandmother. My boyfriend, Chad, and I have a wonderful afternoon planned." Kelly looked right at Alison when she said Chad's name.

Alison waited for that pang of sadness to come — the one she got whenever Chad Simon came to mind. But hearing her ex-boyfriend's name now left her feeling . . . completely fine. Maybe she was over him at last.

Kelly leaned down to kiss her grandmother on the cheek. Tamara flinched at the touch. "Thank you so much for the tea, Grandmother," Kelly said. "And for listening," she added with a glance in Alison's direction.

Alison smiled sweetly at her cousin as she turned to leave. Kelly might be the more conniving, callous, and calculating of the two, but Alison had the home-turf advantage, and that went a long way. Still, she'd have to stay on her toes if she was going to avoid a second attack on Grandmother Diamond's territory.

Alison gave Kelly her best pageant wave, then moved to the Queen Anne chair opposite her grandmother. There were some things she and Tamara needed to talk about and she wanted to watch Her Highness's face when they discussed them. She waited patiently for the front door to open and close — she didn't need any blond-haired eavesdroppers lingering in the hall.

Chapter Nine

Once she was satisfied that Kelly was out of the house, Alison got right to the point. "My father is gone," she said flatly.

Grandmother Diamond eyed her coolly from the couch. "I know," she replied, pretending to remove a piece of lint from her immaculate wool skirt. "Your Aunt Phoebe called last night while you were out, to give me the news. Your father has decided to check himself into a rehabilitation clinic for his problems with alcohol. Quite wise of him, I must say." She nodded to show her approval.

"Do you know where he is?" Alison prodded.

Tamara was silent for a long moment. "He's

asked us not to tell you. We decided that it is best if you don't know. For now, you are to have no contact with him."

Alison felt a flash of anger and quickly banked it. She was back now and needed to make this work. Still, she wondered, who, exactly, were "we"? She knew her father wouldn't have made that or any other decision with Grandmother Diamond — they hadn't been on speaking terms for years.

A shiver made its way up Alison's spine. It was all too possible that her grandmother had forced her father to agree to the no-contact rule by holding something over him. But what?

Not me, *I hope*, she thought grimly. If only she and her dad had managed to join forces against her grandmother . . . If only they had stuck together after her mother's arrest, instead of each retreating into different worlds — her dad to his drinking, Alison to her grandmother's mansion — they might have been able to help each other through this.

Alison swallowed to keep down the bile rising in her throat. If she lost her temper, her grandmother would only reprimand her on top of everything else. Tamara Diamond did not like shows of emotion. Her face was like a mask, as usual. Alison could see where her mother got her great skill for "Looking Good," her trademark posture of efficiency and style.

"Do you know what happened to all of our stuff?" Alison asked through tight lips.

Tamara cocked a well-groomed brow. "He sold the furnishings?" She answered the question with a question. Then, blinking slowly, she nodded. "Of course, he needed money for the clinic. What a pity."

Alison gulped again. Never again seeing the stuff she grew up with was more than just a "pity." And selling it off was more than her dad could have handled alone.

"Why didn't Dad call me himself? Why didn't he call my cell phone?" Alison asked pointedly.

"He didn't want to upset you, of course," Tamara said evenly. "He knows how much you've been through and didn't want to make things any worse."

Yeah, because disappearing when I need him certainly makes things better, Alison thought bitterly. *And having my room trashed isn't at all disturbing.* Outwardly she set her jaw and nodded, as if she agreed with the decision. She needed to act as if this information satisfied all her concerns.

"Thank you for telling me," Alison said, getting to her feet. "I think I'll go straighten my room." It was the first time she'd acknowledged the ransacking — and she was basically letting Her Highness know she was prepared to swallow that bitter pill without choking.

If she was going to stay on her grandmother's good side — and she knew that was her best, and maybe only, option — she had to act as though she was grateful for everything Tamara did for her. Especially now that Kelly was angling for the favorite granddaughter position. Playing along with what Grandmother Diamond wanted was the best way to stay in her graces. And if she could lie low but stay alert, she might still be able to find out what was really happening with her dad.

"Good girl," Tamara said, acknowledging her granddaughter's acquiesence. "Better to bend than to break," she said, referring to one of her favorite adages about the resilience of willow trees.

"I'll see you at dinner, Grandmother," Alison said, as she left the room. She had a lot of cleaning and unpacking to do — it looked like she would be staying under her grandmother's roof for a little while longer.

Chapter Ten

Tom grabbed a tray and slid it along the rail that lined the hot food station in the Stafford Academy lunchroom. The new girl, X, was right in front of him, dressed in a school uniform like she was every day, even though Stafford didn't require uniforms. On anyone else, the fashion statement would seem bizarre — on X, it was intriguing, just like her name. That was one of the things Tom would have loved to ask her about. Only problem was, he turned into a stammering idiot in her presence. "Hello, Tomas," she greeted smoothly.

Tom blushed. X had a way of making guys do that. She was as beautiful as she was mysterious.

"Hey," Tom replied as he grabbed some silverware.

"What the — ?" He looked down at the spoon in his hand and realized that it was dirty. A glop of brown gunk slipped off of it and stuck to his finger. Gross. Tom felt a flash of anger and shook his hand furiously. "Get off of me!" he said loudly. Ugh. Why did this stuff always happen to him? He swiped furiously at his sticky finger with a napkin.

"Need some hand sanitizer?" a husky voice purred in his ear. Tom didn't need to look to know that it was Audra. It was always Audra — all Audra, all the time. Ever since the reception it seemed like every time he turned around, there she was. But it wasn't so bad, really. He was actually kind of flattered by the way she was so fixated on him.

Even though he had no romantic interest in Audra whatsoever, Tom had to admit that he kind of liked her. She might be weird, but she was never boring. And unlike everyone else in his life, Tom could say whatever he wanted to her — absolutely anything — and she took it in. He never felt like he needed to impress her, or that she wanted him to be a certain way. He never felt like she was judging him on the way he looked or acted or talked. It was totally refreshing, and much needed. Kind of like the hand sanitizer she was holding out to him right that minute.

"Yeah," he replied, lifting his defiled hand. Audra squirted a small dollop of pale green gel onto his finger, and Tom felt better immediately. He was even glad Audra was strange enough to carry hand sanitizer around. A month ago, he wouldn't have been caught dead socializing with a weirdo like her in the lunchroom. But a lot had changed in the past few weeks. "Thanks," he said when the microbial killer had evaporated. He wiped his purified hand on a napkin before moving up the line and grabbing a bowl of chili and some corn bread.

"No sweat." Audra slid into line behind him and dropped her voice. "Now you can do *me* a little favor," she said darkly. "I want you to tell your sister to watch her step. She's in way over her head." Tom looked up and saw Zoey staring at the two of them from the back of the line. Audra was seriously glaring back. Apparently things between them were heating up. Tom bristled — he did not want to get involved. He was not into passing along threats, especially to family members — even if he didn't care much about them. He considered telling Audra to drop it — she should just get over her stupid brainiac competition — then checked himself. Why should he defend Zoey? She certainly wasn't doing anything for him. He simply nodded. Maybe he'd pass along the message, maybe he wouldn't.

"Need a ride today?" Audra asked easily, as if the whole Zoey thing had never come up. That was one of the nice things about her — she was always moving on to something else. She didn't dwell on any one thing for long — other than him. "I'll find you after school," she added before Tom could answer. Then she raised her eyebrows to say "see ya." She knew better than to follow Tom to his regular spot in the lunchroom. It was strictly A-list.

Tom turned toward his table in time to see Chad pulling a chair out for Kelly. She looked great in her tight black skirt and zip-up sweater. Better than great, actually. She looked . . .

amazing. Tom wondered how the universe could have produced such a perfect creature. And how his best friend had managed to catch her before he did — especially since Chad had belonged to Alison at the time. As Tom crossed to their table, he felt a stab of jealous anger. Why had Chad's life turned out to be so freaking perfect when Tom's was such a mess? It was all he could do to stop himself from walking over and punching the stupid smile off Chad's face. He reached the table and plunked his tray down abruptly, knocking it into Chad's soda.

"Hey, watch it!" Chad complained, as the Pepsi splashed onto his pants.

No, you watch it, Tom thought as he yanked out his chair and sat down.

Kelly leaned across the table toward Tom, and he felt his face grow warm like it always did when she got close. "I see we've got a new shadow," Kelly teased, cocking her head toward Audra, who had planted herself two tables away with a clear view of Tom and his friends. She had been sitting there all week instead of at her usual spot with the debate team.

Tom glowered. "It's nothing," he snapped.

"Whatever." Kelly laughed easily, then pushed back her chair and stood up. "Excuse me, boys. You'll have to entertain yourselves for a bit."

Tom looked away as Kelly tousled Chad's curly hair, then sashayed off to the bathroom.

"Hey, Tom," Chad said. "Are you all right?"

"Yeah. Fine," Tom shot back, irritated. "Never been better."

"You just seem a little —"

"What do you want, Chad?" Tom asked abruptly. "Do you need to copy some homework or something? Just ask, so I can eat my lunch in peace."

"Well, actually," Chad said sheepishly, "I was going to ask if I could just look at your answers for Trig. I was going to do it last night after dinner, but then Kelly called, and . . ." Chad smiled lamely.

And you had something better to do with your time, Tom thought. *Well, guess what, buddy, so do I.*

Tom rifled through his bag, pretending to search for the right assignment. Finally he pulled out a notebook page — it was the problem set from the week before. "Here you go." He smiled as he thrust the paper into Chad's hand.

"Thanks," Chad said.

"No problem." It was time to teach Chad a lesson.

Chapter Eleven

Kelly leaned toward the mirror in the girls'
bathroom and smoothed on her new MAC eye
shadow. She was glad to have a little moment to
herself. She couldn't believe what a bore Tom
was being. He was such a grump that it wasn't
even any fun to tease him about that whack job
Audra. What was he so preoccupied with? He
hadn't even flirted with her when he came to the
table. What was up with that?

Smoothing on a toasty lip stain, Kelly changed
boy subjects in her head, moving on to Chad. He
looked pretty hot today in his jeans and Banana
Republic cashmere sweater. Her good-hearted

decision to keep him in spite of his family secret was turning out to be the right call.

Kelly had almost ditched Chad on the spot when she first found out about Will, his autistic little brother. Kelly Diamond Reeves did not associate with freaks. But instead of bolting, she had played the understanding girlfriend, even going so far as to sit in an ice-cream parlor with the kid. And it had paid off — Chad was now even more sickeningly devoted to her than before. And every time he looked at Kelly with adoration in his puppy-dog eyes, Kelly hoped Alison felt it like a stab through her heart.

"Just wait until Alison sees what's next," Kelly told her reflection with a sly smile as she slid the glossy topcoat over her lips. She was quite sure that Alison had no idea that her ex-boyfriend Chad even *had* a little brother. And Kelly had every intention of being the one to break the news — when the time was right, of course. The fact that Chad had shared his deepest secret with Kelly, not Alison, was sure to crush her.

That news ought to make her even jumpier, Kelly thought. Her cousin had seemed totally uneasy at school lately — a fact Kelly was thoroughly enjoying. She attributed Alison's state to Kelly's recent appearance at Grandmother Diamond's. She'd have to plan another one soon. . . .

Just then the door opened and who should appear but Alison herself.

"Well, well," Kelly said, smiling. "If it isn't Grandmother Diamond's little lapdog." She gave her cousin the once-over, taking note of Alison's new Miu Miu boots and Kashmere shrug. Apparently being Her Highness's favorite was still paying off, at least in terms of Alison's wardrobe.

Alison pretended to ignore her as she turned on the faucet and washed her hands. Kelly smirked. She had no intention of letting Alison off that easy.

"How are they treating you at the Diamond Reformatory? Has the headmistress properly modified your behavior? Are you all set for re-release into society?"

Alison blanched as she turned off the water and reached for some paper towels. "No," she blurted.

Kelly felt the thrill of victory. Were Alison's hands actually shaking? *Get a life, girl! Or better yet, don't.* "Don't worry, cousin," Kelly purred. "Grandmother Diamond and I will put our heads together during our next teatime. We'll have a plan for your future in no time."

Chapter Twelve

Chad leaned against his locker. "Have you seen Tom?" he asked Kelly as he scoped out the hall. The bell had rung five minutes ago, and Tom was nowhere to be seen. He and Tom were supposed to hang out today, and Chad had been looking forward to it. What with all the time he spent with Kelly, and taking care of his little brother, Will, and Tom doing stuff for his dad's wedding, Chad felt like they had barely seen each other lately. They needed to catch up.

"Not since lunch," Kelly replied, studying her face in the mirror she kept inside her locker door. "Do you think I should color my hair? I'm thinking about getting highlights."

"You'd look great with highlights — but you already look great without them," Chad said dutifully. He closed his eyes and rubbed his temples. His head was aching again.

"Really?" Kelly asked, pouting a little.

"Really." Chad smiled and leaned in, grazing his lips across her forehead and getting a good whiff of her hair. It smelled even better than it looked. Chad breathed in, feeling like the luckiest guy in the world. But as he pulled away, his heart caught in his throat. Across the hall, Alison was taking her coat out of her locker.

Chad forced himself to look back at Kelly, who was still preening away. Ever since he'd gotten that nasty nosebleed a couple weeks ago and Alison had helped him to the nurse, his heart sped up a little whenever he saw her.

It's just guilt, Chad assured himself. After all, he had broken up with her only a couple of days after her mom was arrested. He'd *had* to do it then, before she had the chance to break up with him first. Kelly had told him more than once that Alison was getting ready to dump him. Still, the whole thing had been humiliating for Alison. Anybody with a heart would feel bad about that. He was just feeling sorry for her, right?

As Chad watched Alison gather her books together, conflicting emotions crashed inside him like ocean waves against the rocky base of a cliff. But the sudden slam of Kelly's locker door snapped him out of it, and fast. Kelly had seen who he was staring at . . . and she was scowling. Chad felt like pond scum for a moment, but then Kelly stepped closer and smiled sweetly. "How is Will?" she asked, looking over her shoulder and lowering her voice. Chad was grateful for her discretion. It was good to know she could keep a secret, especially since nobody else at school, except Tom, knew about his autistic little brother — and that's the way Chad wanted to keep it. He wasn't ashamed of Will. But at Stafford, appearance and reputation were everything, and most people didn't understand about autism. They freaked out when they saw Will hitting himself and flapping his hands and making weird noises. They thought he was some kind of freak, even though he was anything but. Will was totally smart. He loved to memorize facts, figures, and bus maps. And though he didn't show it the way other people did, he was supersensitive. Thankfully, and a little surprisingly, Kelly was great with Will.

Chad had totally panicked when Kelly had spotted him and Will in the Doggie Dog parking lot last week. He'd had no intention of telling her about his little brother — ever. Why should he? He'd never told Alison, and they'd been together for ages. Like his other little secrets — that he could only afford Stafford because he was on a full scholarship, and he could only keep his scholarship because Tom helped him keep up his grades. Tom was the only person who knew because Chad wanted him to. Tom was a totally solid best friend, and Chad could trust him with anything — even his life. He must have had a good reason to stand him up today, like a family emergency. Or maybe he just spaced. The poor guy really had a lot on his mind.

Chad put his arm around his girlfriend. "Will? He's doing all right," he said, pleased that it was true. Will had been pretty calm ever since Kelly had taken them both out for ice cream. He had not had a major episode in a week. Sure, it might have had more to do with the fact that the boys' older brother, Dustin, had been kicked out of the house, which had cut way back on the fighting. But Chad preferred to think Will's newfound calm was because his new girlfriend was magic.

"Hey, since it looks like Tom is standing me up, you want to go get some ice cream with your two favorite boys?" Chad asked. "Will would love to see you."

Kelly's smile faded. "Oh, I can't," she said. "But I'll call you later, okay?" She gave Chad a quick squeeze, then slipped away from him and headed down the Stafford hall. Her Emilio Pucci heels clicked quietly on the stone floor.

A smile spread across Chad's face as he watched her go. She was so sweet and so beautiful. The nagging feeling he'd had over Alison a moment before was gone. Kelly was the best girlfriend a guy could hope for.

Chapter Thirteen

Leaning back against the leather seat of the taxi, Alison played with the silver key on the thin chain around her neck. She still had no idea what it unlocked — she just knew that it was her only link to her father. She'd been wearing it for almost two weeks, keeping it on her at all times, even when she showered or slept, just in case. There was no way she was going to lose this, too. Shutting her eyes, she wondered if her mother knew what was going on. She was afraid to hope so, but could not help it. It was unlikely that Jack would have visited his wife before he vanished, but even in jail, Helen Rose was powerful enough to get whatever information she wanted.

Except out of Grandmother Diamond . . . or me, Alison thought with more than a touch of guilt. Before her father disappeared, her mother had asked Alison to do some snooping. It was the reason she had discovered the documents that were now hidden at Zoey's. But after Alison found them, she was not sure what she wanted to do with them, and she'd never told her mother what she'd found in Grandmother Diamond's secret vault. Now Alison knew she could never tell. She had no choice but to keep the stolen documents under wraps. Her Highness had made it far too clear that Alison couldn't risk making an enemy out of her, especially since revealing the documents wouldn't necessarily guarantee Alison's mom's release. For all Alison knew, Grandmother Diamond could have already bought off the judge and the jury. And even though Tamara certainly was guilty of meddling, that didn't mean Helen Rose was innocent of all charges. Alison was trapped — still, she felt terribly guilty about it. Her mother had asked Alison to stand by her, to help her, and what was she doing? Nothing.

A hopeless feeling welled up inside of Alison,

with anger hot on its heels. This whole situation was a nightmare.

As the taxi made its way up the drive to the jail, something caught Alison's eye. An elderly woman with stiff, proud posture and an expensive fur coat was getting into a Rolls-Royce at the visitor's exit. It was a very familiar Rolls-Royce, and an even more familiar woman. Tamara Diamond.

"Please stop right here," Alison told the driver abruptly. She didn't want her grandmother to see her. And more important, she didn't want Grandmother Diamond to know that she had been seen. As the Rolls-Royce sped past, Alison crouched down in the backseat of the cab. She could feel the blood pounding in her ears and she felt a little like a Dalmatian puppy hiding from Cruella DeVil.

"Someone out to get you?" the taxi driver joked. Alison reached into her Fendi wallet and pulled out a few bills — a tiny fraction of the generous allowance Tamara had been giving her.

"Sometimes I think so," she replied grimly, handing over the money. Feeling like she was moving in slow motion, she grabbed her coat and stepped out of the cab, giving the door a good slam. What the heck was her grandmother doing visiting her mother in jail? That had to be why Tamara was there, but she and Helen had barely spoken since before Alison was born. They were sworn enemies!

Or were they? Alison began to wonder as she walked up to the prison entrance. She nearly staggered as a terrifying thought hit her like a landslide: Everything she had ever known about her mother and grandmother's relationship could be a complete lie. So much else in their family was a secret or a deception. Why not this, too?

Her mind reeling, Alison walked past the guards and gates to the visitor sign-in. *Maybe she came to tell my mom about my dad's disappearance,* she thought, desperate for a reasonable explanation. *I'm sure Her Highness would love to deliver yet more bad news to Mom behind bars. . . .* She scribbled her name in the visitor's log, scanning it for Tamara Diamond's name. She didn't see it. She passed through several locked doors until she was admitted into the waiting room. By the time she got to take a seat across from her mother she was trembling so badly she knew she wouldn't be able to speak normally. She stared at her mother through the thick glass between them for several long moments, trying to calm down. Helen Rose was composed on the other side of the glass, waiting.

Finally, Alison picked up the phone. "What was Grandmother Diamond doing here?" she choked out.

On the other side of the glass, Helen's face tightened almost imperceptibly. But she shook her head and assumed an expression of innocence. "I don't know what you're talking about," she replied. Her tone suggested that the very idea was ridiculous.

Alison gaped openly. She couldn't help it, and she didn't care if her expression irritated or offended her mother. How could she lie to her so easily and obviously after everything that had happened? Was she even human? Did she even care the tiniest bit about Alison, her only child? Could she be trusted at all, *ever*?

"That's it?" Alison practically shouted.

"You're just going to sit there and deny it? I *saw* her outside! I watched her walk out, get into her car, and get whisked away! I *know* she was here!"

Helen stared evenly at her daughter, without flinching. Her eyes looked almost amused. As Alison stared back, she suddenly realized that her mother looked good today. Her short auburn hair had been cut recently and she looked composed and well rested. Had she been expecting Tamara's visit? Had the meeting been some kind of victory for Helen? Alison couldn't even imagine what secrets her mother and her grandmother were hiding, or what kind of game they were playing. All she knew was that she was furious at both of them.

"Dad is gone," Alison blurted harshly, watching for a reaction — any reaction — on her mother's face. She hoped the news was a blow, even though that would mean that her mother couldn't tell her what was going on.

Helen waved a hand through the air dismissively. "Oh, Jack, how typical," she murmured. Then she sighed heavily, as if explaining this to Alison was a burden. "Your father is many things, Alison, but reliable is not one of them.

That's why I asked you to keep an eye on him until I'm released. He's just not capable of taking care of himself. Don't worry, he's probably just off on a drinking binge. He'll turn up. Hopefully before the press finds him."

Alison felt as fragile as a sweater with a giant snag. One more tug and she would unravel in a major way. She couldn't tell if her father's disappearance was news to her mother or not. Helen certainly didn't seem to be taking it seriously. But if she and Grandmother Diamond were in on this together, they'd neglected to get their cover story straight. Alison suddenly felt like her dad was even farther away. "No, Mom. This is not just a binge. He's gone. The house is empty. His phone is disconnected. It's been over a week." She considered telling her mother Tamara's explanation but decided against it. There was no way of knowing if it were true. Alison felt her eyes misting up. "Please tell me you know where he is," she practically begged. "Please tell me he's okay, and that you know when he's coming back."

Helen's expression changed to one of concern — an expression Alison rarely saw on her mother's face. "What do you mean, the house is empty?" she asked, leaning closer to the glass.

"I mean the house is empty," Alison replied evenly. It was so typical that her mother cared more about her belongings than about her husband — or her daughter. "No furniture, no anything. Everything is gone."

Helen cursed under her breath so quietly that Alison wasn't sure she'd actually heard the words.

"Mom," Alison said, getting back to what mattered. "Please tell me what you know about Dad."

Helen stared at Alison for a long time, like she was trying to read her daughter's thoughts. Then she shook her head, and her blue eyes looked empty. "I can't, Alison," she said quietly. "Because I don't know a thing."

Chapter Fourteen

Chad set the peanut butter sandwich he'd made for Will down on the table. It was cut into one-inch squares — no jam, no crusts. "Here you go, buddy," he said as Will stabbed each bite with a toothpick before popping it into his mouth. Chad smiled, wishing he had a quarter of his little brother's appetite. Will loved food almost as much as he loved his orange sweatshirt. Lately Chad hadn't been able to stomach much of anything.

"Peanut butter goes with milk." Will began to chant between bites. Chad pulled out the red plastic cup Will always used — the one with a lid on it — and filled it from the jug in the fridge.

Will took it gratefully and put it to the right of his plate, turning it slightly until he had it positioned just right.

While Will ate, Chad took his phone from his pocket. He'd been trying to reach Tom ever since the guy'd blown him off the day before. Hitting speed dial number two for about the seventh time, he waited for the call to go through. Across the kitchen, Will was starting to flap his hands. He needed a straw for his milk. Quickly Chad got him one with his free hand.

The phone didn't even ring before it went to voice mail. Chad snapped his LG shut with a sigh. There was no point in leaving yet another message — he'd already left three. So why hadn't Tom called him back?

Chad rubbed his aching forehead while he tried to think. *Maybe I should just go over to Tom's house,* he thought. If Tom was home they could just hang out for a while. Chad eyed his brother at the table. No, that wouldn't work. He couldn't bring Will with him — most of the world, including Zoey, didn't even know he existed — and he couldn't leave him alone, either. As usual his parents had made weekend plans — separately — and assumed Chad would be home to babysit. Not that Chad minded, really. A day at home with Will and *without* his fighting parents was not a bad deal.

Except that it prevented him from finding Tom, who he was really beginning to worry about. His best friend had been acting pretty weird — ever since his dad's wedding — but hadn't given Chad a clue about what was going on. And what was up with all the time Tom was suddenly spending with Audra? Chad had nothing against the girl, but she was not even close to being in Tom's league.

Chad eyed his phone, willing it to ring. He had a feeling that the sooner he connected with Tom, the better.

Chapter Fifteen

"Get up, *now*," a voice barked from the doorway of Tom's room. "It's almost noon."

Tom opened one eye and saw his father yanking open the window curtains. The sun was glaring harshly down on him. And so was his father. The honeymoon was over — big-time.

Tom shaded his eyes and grudgingly sat up in bed. "And?" he said, not caring if he fueled his father's anger. He was done trying to lie low and keep everything cool.

Tom had spent his whole life scrambling to please his father — trying to do well enough in school and in sports to win his respect. No more. Why should he bust his butt for a man who'd murdered his own wife? The man who'd murdered Tom's mother? Ever since Tom had found that newspaper photo of the scene of his mother's death, showing his father's car — a car his mother was incapable of driving — being pulled out of the lake she'd drowned in, Tom had been certain DA Dad had murdered his mom. And when he had accused his father of the murder at his wedding reception, and his father hadn't even denied it — in Tom's mind it was confirmed. Tom hadn't seen his father since.

Now here he was. Tom glared silently up at his dad, who appeared to be pretending that the conversation at the wedding had never happened. Tom knew better. And he wasn't going to take any more flak from his dad.

Bring it on, Pops. Rant away.

"*And* your room is a mess, there are dishes in the sink, and the lawn needs to be raked," DA Ramirez ticked off the items on his thick fingers before planting his hands on his hips.

Tom rubbed his eyes, ignoring the lecture. "Welcome home, Dad. How was the honeymoon?" he asked sarcastically. It felt good not to care. Really good.

"Don't use that tone with me, Tomas," DA Ramirez hissed. "You're already walking a very thin line. Now get out of bed and get cracking. If you're lucky, you'll be done by dinner." He spun around and stormed toward the door.

"You mean if *you're* lucky," Tom replied as his dad left the room, banging the door open against the wall. "And your luck just ran out," he added. He grabbed his cell off his nightstand and hit Audra's number. He would not take orders from his mother's murderer. He would not even stay in the same house.

"You must have ESP," Audra said when she picked up. "I was just going to call you."

"So what else is new?" Tom cracked. "Listen, I need a ride. How quickly can you get over here?" Tom pulled on his jeans, holding the phone between his ear and shoulder.

Audra laughed. "Look out your window."

Tom glanced out and spotted Audra's car idling across the street in her favorite spot, next to his neighbor's very tall, very manicured privacy hedge. "Nice," he said into the phone. "I'll be right down."

Two minutes later, Tom was sliding into the

now-familiar leather passenger seat of the Audi TT and pulling on his seat belt.

"Hey, thanks for stalking me this morning," Tom half joked as Audra slipped into gear and tore down the tree-lined residential road. She clearly had something against speed limits. "I had to get out of there, fast," he said.

"Zoey problems? I can take care of that if you want," Audra said, sounding dead serious.

Tom shook his head and wondered what that meant exactly. "No, it's not Zoey. We're not talking. It's my dad. He's been home for, like, five minutes and he's already all up in my face about stupid stuff. He is such a colossal jerk." *And a murderer.* Tom pounded his fist on the dashboard. His father had some nerve.

Audra shifted into fifth gear and stepped on the gas. "Don't sweat it. We're already leaving them far behind."

"Good." Tom sat back. "I can always count on you."

"Hey — haven't I been telling you that all along? Nobody understands you like I do, Tom."

Tom snorted. "You really are creepy sometimes, you know that?"

Audra smiled happily. "Anyway, where was Zoey when your dad was getting on your case? Isn't it, like, a sister's *job* to help out when that happens? What are siblings for?"

Tom ran his hands through his hair. "I don't know, man. I don't know."

"How's the bimbo bride?" Audra asked, half-changing the subject. "Living with her must be a total trip. Is there anything on her body that's actually *hers*? I can't believe your dad has developed such shallow taste. I mean, your real mom was so amazing."

Tom's hands froze on his head. "You knew my mom?" he asked quietly, turning to look at Audra.

"Well, not really," Audra admitted with a casual shrug. "My dad did, though. He was her shrink."

Tom's hands dropped to his lap. *Whoa.* He tried to process this surprise information, but it was too much for his startled brain.

"He treated her for years. Probably knew her better than anyone," Audra said. "And, you know, sometimes I help my dad with the filing. That was how I learned about you, actually." She said all this as casually as if she were explaining what she'd eaten for breakfast. Tom just listened, stunned. "Believe me, most of the cases are dull as dishwater. But your mom! She was fascinating. So tormented!"

Tom flinched.

"The smartest people always are, you know," Audra said, as if reassuring Tom. "Tormented, I mean. Anyway, I could tell by my dad's notes that he thought the world of her. And she thought the world of you."

Tom felt dizzy as he gazed at the yellow lines rolling under the Audi TT. They were disappearing way too fast, like Tom's grip on things. Audra was talking about his *mom*. The one he'd lost. The one he missed so much it made his chest ache.

Audra shouldn't know that stuff, Tom thought suddenly. He felt like his mom's privacy — and *his* privacy — had been seriously violated.

Audra has the file . . . he thought, still trying to wrap his brain around the whole situation. Maybe it wasn't such a terrible thing. Maybe the stuff his mom had told her shrink could help him figure out what had actually happened —

how she really died. Tom took a breath. "Can I see it?" he asked, trying to sound casual. "Can you get me her file?"

Audra smiled wickedly. "Maybe," she replied. "But it will cost you."

"Cost me what?" Tom asked, ready to pay any price.

"Twelve hours," Audra said. "Starting right now. You're coming with me."

Tom suddenly realized they were driving up the on-ramp to the highway. "Come with you where?"

Audra took her hands off the wheel and held them up like she was riding a roller coaster. Then she shrieked and grabbed the wheel again, making the car swerve. "Everywhere!" she shouted. "Full speed ahead!"

Chapter Sixteen

Alison rolled over in bed and reached for her ringing cell. Only one person would call her before ten on a Sunday morning — Zoey.

"Hey," she said with a yawn. "What's up?"

Before Zoey could even answer, Alison could hear what was up. Tom and his dad were screaming at each other in the background. "Whoa," Alison said. It sounded pretty intense.

"No kidding," Zoey replied. "And that's round two, coming from behind a closed door. Tom didn't get home until three o'clock this morning. Dad was like a tiger the whole time he was gone, and when Tom finally showed, he pounced. They were at each other's throats for an hour, and Tom kept saying weird stuff like 'the secret's out' and 'I'm not going to listen to advice about my life from the jerk who destroyed it.' What is that supposed to mean?"

Alison shook her head. "No clue."

"Now they're back at it. I'm not sure they're ever going to stop. . . ."

"Oh, Zoey." Alison winced. She felt terrible for Zoey — and for Tom. He worked hard in school and played varsity lacrosse in the spring. He did well at everything he tried, but it was never good enough for his dad.

Alison twirled a lock of hair as Zoey bombarded her with fight details. She was listening but slightly distracted by something else — a twinge of jealousy. Audra certainly seemed to be spending a lot of time with Tom lately. She didn't seem to be his girlfriend or anything — Alison had noticed that Tom still spent his lunch period with Kelly and Chad and she'd never seen Tom and Audra so much as hold hands — but they definitely appeared to be getting closer and closer, even as Tom was pushing everyone else in his life further away. Alison was surprised to find herself wishing that *she* were the one Tom was turning to, instead of Audra. Though she'd never admitted it to anyone — especially Zoey — Alison thought Tom was pretty great. Maybe it was his sense of humor. Maybe it was his deep, dark eyes. Whatever the reason, Alison had a soft spot for him.

He's such a good guy, Alison thought. *And Audra is a little . . .*

"Hey, are you even listening to me?" Zoey asked, interrupting Alison's thoughts.

"Sorry. It's just, I'm feeling kinda bad for your brother. It seems like he's really been spiraling lately. You know, downward. I've been there, and it stinks. Having a parent come down on you when you're already so low can be a bad mix."

"Are you kidding?" Zoey said incredulously. "I can't believe I'm going to say this, but I think my dad is right on target this time." There was silence on both ends of the line for a second. Then Zoey said darkly, "Seriously, Al. Someone has to reel him in, before he goes too far. The whole Audra thing isn't helping. She's out there, you know? And I just wish that he'd listen to somebody a little more sane, like *me*."

"I'm sorry, Zo," Alison said softly. "You're right." She wished there was something she could do to help. "Oh, no. I have to go," she said, glancing at the clock. "Kelly's family is coming for brunch and I have to get ready. I can't give the evil cousin any opportunity to gain ground with Her Highness."

"Right," Zoey said knowingly. "Knock 'em dead."

Alison laughed. "If only," she replied.

Snapping the phone shut, she stepped into her walk-in closet and eyed her clothing options. She wanted to look well dressed but not dressed up. That would be too obvious, especially to Kelly.

After a couple of bad starts, she pulled on a pair of Miss Sixty skinny jeans and layered two jewel-tone paper-thin Hayden cashmere sweaters on top. Slipping her feet into her Delman embellished ballet flats, she grabbed the brush from her dressing table and gave her hair a few good strokes before messing it up just enough. A fresh coat of lip gloss and a light touch of mascara later, she was ready for battle.

Chapter Seventeen

Alison checked the clock and hurried down the stairs. It was still a little early, but she knew her grandmother valued promptness. She was feeling fit for the fight until she walked into the dining room. Kelly was already there, alone, looking fabulous, and seated in Alison's chair.

"So glad you could make it," Kelly remarked snidely. "As you know, it's leftovers for the late-comers." She gestured toward the seat across from her — the one Kelly usually sat in. Although that seat was also right next to Grandmother Diamond's, sitting there would be a definite demotion for Alison. Being on their grand-mother's left, rather than on her right, meant that Alison would be the last person to be served or cleared. It was also symbolic — Alison had held the right-hand seat of honor for as long as she and Kelly had been old enough to join the grown-ups at the dinner table, rather than eating with the servants in the kitchen. But Alison couldn't let Kelly see that she cared.

Slowly taking the bad seat, Alison stared her cousin down. She would not look away or blink first. "Do you really think that stealing my seat is going to change the way Grandmother Diamond feels about you, Kelly?" she said evenly. "I'm still her favorite, and it's still *my* seat. Don't forget, I actually *live* here."

Kelly smiled cruelly. "And that's supposed to make me jealous? Thanks, but I'd rather live in a house where I get to call the shots. You know, instead of having to kiss up to someone I hate because she's got me cornered."

Alison swallowed hard. Kelly's words could not be more true. Or more depressing. But she had to hold her chin high — not let it show. Where was her zinging retort? Alison was trying to think of one when Grandmother Diamond entered the dining room flanked by Kelly's parents, Phoebe and Bill.

Alison jumped to her feet and pulled out her grandmother's chair, leaning Tamara's gold-topped cane against the wall nearby. Tamara unbuttoned the top button of her perfectly tailored, collarless wool blazer before she sat down. "Thank you, Alison," she said as Alison pushed her chair in. She raised an eyebrow at Kelly on her right. "Playing musical chairs, dear?"

Alison smirked as Kelly looked down at her empty china plate without responding.

Before the platter of eggs Benedict with salmon had even reached Alison, Kelly struck back. "Did you catch the morning talk shows today, Alison? I wonder how they found out that your father is missing."

Alison felt a sharp lump in her throat. No, she *hadn't* seen the coverage of this latest twist in Helen Rose's national scandal — but she'd be willing to place a pretty high wager that whoever tipped off the media about her dad's disappearance was related to her by blood.

"Kelly!" Aunt Phoebe clucked. She pretended

she didn't want to upset Alison. But then she couldn't resist giving details herself. "It's all over the news," Aunt Phoebe said, fiddling with her ruby brooch and looking concerned. "And on the front of today's paper . . ."

"It's horrifying what the Rose family has been reduced to," Grandmother Diamond announced, inhaling through her nose. "Not just one, but both of them splashed all over the media."

Alison stared down at her lap to avoid Kelly's triumphant look.

"Well," Kelly's father, Bill, said, "at least Christine is keeping herself out of the limelight for the time being."

"Don't hold your breath," Grandmother Diamond sneered. "Christine will do anything for publicity."

Across the table, Kelly's face looked a little pinched, and Alison smiled. It was true that their movie star aunt loved attention — any kind — and Alison savored the fact that the mention of Christine's name still upset her cousin.

"Let's look at the silver lining, shall we?" Aunt

Phoebe chirped. "At least Jack won't be here for the trial."

Alison's head shot up. What was that supposed to mean? Was Aunt Phoebe *glad* that Alison's dad might not be at the trial to support her mom?

"Indeed." Grandmother Diamond nodded as she took a sip of her mimosa. "Pity for Helen, of course. But the last thing we need is an extra act in the courtroom circus. But surely we can find a more pleasant conversation topic for a Sunday morning."

Alison pushed the eggs around on her plate and tuned out the rest of the discussion. Was that the real reason why someone had wanted her father to disappear? To deal her mother an emotional blow during the trial? Was it really worth all the trouble of erasing him from Alison's life, just to deliver that petty setback to Helen? If Grandmother Diamond was indeed responsible for Jack's absence and that was her motivation, why hadn't she delivered the news to Helen herself during their mysterious visit? Alison's mind reeled, and her stomach sank. It was all too much. She felt completely, overwhelmingly helpless. Kelly had been right — Grandmother Diamond had her cornered.

Alison was thoroughly relieved when Tamara dismissed everyone from the table, announcing that a fire and hot tea would be ready in the parlor in ten minutes. She could not take another second of Kelly's smug face.

"A ten-minute break is better than nothing," Alison murmured to herself as she headed for the stairs. But Kelly intercepted her in the hall.

"No Daddy, either?" she jabbed. "Poor little Alison might be stuck living here forever."

"Whatever," Alison said. She didn't have the energy for a fight.

"Not whatever, *for*ever," Kelly corrected.

Alison ignored the words and pushed past her cousin. She took the stairs two at a time and was making a beeline down the corridor to her room when voices made her stop. Her grandmother's bedroom door was ajar, and she was speaking to someone inside.

"Well done, Phoebe," Tamara said. "Though I must admit, I should not be so surprised. You always have excelled at cleaning up messes."

Alison stood stock-still outside the slightly open door. Her grandmother *never* complimented Aunt Phoebe.

"He *is* a mess, isn't he?" Phoebe replied with a girlish giggle. "Well, that only made it easier to get rid of him. I, for one, am sleeping better with him tucked away. It bought us some time, at least, before the truth gets out."

Alison's heart pounded as she hurried to her room. As she closed the door she sank to the carpet. She knew full well who Aunt Phoebe and Grandmother Diamond had been referring to. The biggest mess in the family was none other than her father, Jack Rose.

What secret he held or threatened, she had no idea, but at least she knew now there were *two* keys to this mystery: the small, silver one on the chain around her neck, and Aunt Phoebe.

Chapter Eighteen

Zoey pulled a couple of textbooks out of her messenger bag and dumped them into her locker. It was Monday morning, her father and his bimbo wife were back, and the blowup between Tom and their dad was still not over. They were so mad at each other it seemed like there would never be peace in the house again.

Not that the "peace" before was actually that peaceful, she reminded herself grimly. No, home life had pretty much bit since she'd gotten home from boarding school number five. No wait, since her mom had died.

Resigning herself to another day at the prestigious Stafford Academy, Zoey scanned the hall for Alison, who she hadn't seen yet. She needed a glimpse of her best friend to cheer her up, or to at least let her know that she was not alone in her misery.

Zoey turned to look over her shoulder just as Audra appeared out of nowhere, her face in a snarl. "Think you're so smart?" she growled. "So important? Well, I know better, and so does everyone else . . . including your brother."

Zoey stepped back, putting her bag between herself and Audra and trying not to flinch. Audra was so close she could feel tiny flecks of spit hitting her face.

"Back off, freakfest," Zoey said, glaring at Audra from behind her fringed bangs. "What's your problem?"

"The valedictorian spot is mine," Audra hissed as she turned away. "Just like your brother."

Zoey watched her go, her heart hammering in her chest. Was it just her or was Audra getting seriously scary?

Chapter Nineteen

"Hey, man." Chad set his tray down at the usual table and sank into the chair across from Tom. He was totally wiped. But as tired as he was, he was really glad to find Tom alone. He hoped Kelly would take her time at the salad bar. He and Tom needed a chance to talk.

Except that Tom didn't reply, or even look up from his hamburger.

"What's up?" Chad leaned in, trying to catch Tom's eye. "I thought we were supposed to hang out Friday."

Finally Tom looked up. He shot Chad an unmistakable "are you kidding?" look. "What?"

Tom put his hand to his ear like he was hard of hearing. "What's that you're whining about?" He pulled his hand down and waved it at Chad like he was brushing away a fly. "You've been blowing me off ever since you hooked up with Kelly." He snorted. "It's about time you tasted some of what you dish out."

Chad froze with his sandwich raised halfway to his mouth. Tom had been nursing some attitude lately, but this seemed completely out of left field. What right did *he* have to be mad? He wasn't the one who'd been stood up. And bringing up Kelly was totally unfair.

But what Tom said next made Chad drop his sandwich back on his plate.

"Aw, don't worry your pretty head." Tom's voice dripped with sarcasm. "I'll still let you copy my homework — that's all you really need from me, right?"

The two boys' eyes locked, Chad's wide and Tom's narrowed. Chad was shocked to see genuine hatred in his best friend's gaze. He had no idea what to say. Where was this coming from? Yeah, lately he'd needed a little more help with his homework than usual, but Tom had never acted like it was a big deal before. They had been best friends for years. Friends helped each other out all the time . . . didn't they? Did Tom want him to end up in public high school? They were supposed to graduate *together* in two years.

Anger and guilt swirled together inside of Chad. He could not deny that Kelly had been the biggest thing on his mind lately. And after that came Will . . . and Dustin . . . and his parents fighting . . . and Alison . . . and keeping up with school. He had so much going on, maybe he *had* been taking Tom for granted a little. Not on purpose, though! And he wasn't using him. He would never do that to his best friend.

Only Tom thought he was doing exactly that. He thought Chad didn't care. And if Chad didn't fix that, fast, it could get out of hand.

"Whoa. Tom, listen. It's not about the homework and it never has been. You're my *best friend*."

"Whatever you tell yourself," Tom growled.

Chad opened his mouth to try again and saw Tom's eyes lock on something behind him. Turning, he saw Kelly carrying her tray to their table. The rest of this conversation would have to wait.

Chapter Twenty

Kelly stood next to the table holding her tray and waiting for *someone* to pull out her chair. "Hellooo," she said in an "anybody home?" sort of voice. Boys could be so oblivious. Sometimes it was more work to wake them up than to do things yourself. Slamming her tray down next to Chad, she yanked out her own chair with a sigh and sat down. "Don't worry. I'll get it," she grumbled.

"Sorry." Chad smiled at her sheepishly before staring back at his uneaten sandwich and fries. Tom didn't even look up. What was with these guys? This was lunch, not a funeral. And Kelly was in no mood to be ignored. If her boys weren't going to entertain her, someone else was going to have to step up to the plate.

Scanning the cafeteria, Kelly's eyes landed on the perfect amusement. Audra Wilson — Tom's little shadow. She was sitting in her new regular spot, two tables away, staring at Tom like he was her precious puppy let loose in the park. The girl clearly thought she owned him. It was laughable. Audra didn't even try to hide how crazy she was for Tom. Or how crazy she was, period.

For several long minutes, Kelly watched Audra gaze possessively at Tom. Finally Audra noticed Kelly looking. Kelly smiled fakely, squinched up her nose, and waggled her fingers in a wave. Audra stared daggers.

Wow. Kelly was impressed by the edgy venom in Audra's look. *Is she seriously crazy enough to take me on?* Nobody *ever* chose to take Kelly on. No one except her annoying blackmailer TT. . . . Luckily, Kelly hadn't heard from "Truthteller" in a while — not since she'd made that $500 payment.

Wait a second . . . Kelly's mind raced as the girls stared at each other, unmoving and unblinking. Could Audra be her blackmailer? It seemed like a possibility. Kelly had never really given the girl much thought before, but she definitely seemed like the type. Kelly was certain Audra didn't need the money — her dad was a shrink with a pretty exclusive client list — but she seemed crazy enough to pull that kind of stunt just for fun. Well, if Audra was Kelly's black-mailer, the revenge was about to begin.

Certain that Audra would keep watching, Kelly turned her attention to Tom. She flashed him her winning smile. "So, Tom — did you do anything fun last weekend?"

Tom looked flustered. "Not really. I, uh, went for a long drive. Slept in a bit." Kelly nodded encouragingly and Tom visibly relaxed. "What about you?"

Kelly laughed for Audra's benefit. "Oh, you know . . . long, boring brunch at Grandmother Diamond's on Sunday. Shopping on Saturday, and a movie with Chad."

"You look really great today," Tom said, glancing at Chad as he said it. "I like that color on you. It really brings out your eyes."

"You think?" Kelly gushed, giving him a slow blink. This was the kind of attention she had been waiting for, and deserved. She hoped Chad was taking note. Audra definitely was. Leaning across the table, Kelly lifted her napkin and wiped an imaginary dab of mustard off Tom's chin. "You're a mess," she scolded coyly. "Cute, though." She winked. "How come you don't have a girlfriend, Tom?"

Chad's head jerked up but Kelly did not look away. She went on smiling into Tom's eyes, completely aware that they had a rapt audience of two.

Chapter Twenty-one

Strutting across the parking lot after school, Kelly felt unusually fabulous. Her lunchroom flirtation with Tom had put her in a great mood. It was seriously the most fun she'd had at school since —

The sudden screech of tires and the screams of the girls around her wiped the smile off of Kelly's flawless face. A shiny silver Audi squealed to a halt just inches away from her knee-high Prada boots. Kelly stood frozen, barely able to breathe. The smell of burnt rubber filled her nose. Looking up, she stared through the windshield of the car at the driver who had almost mowed her down. Audra returned her gaze, unabashed and unapologetic. The late-afternoon light glinted off her glasses. She looked unmistakably smug.

Kelly was speechless. Audra had nearly run her down! And there was no doubt she'd done it on purpose. That girl was a psychopath.

Still rooted to the spot, Kelly seethed. She could have been killed . . . or worse, maimed.

For what felt like several long moments, neither girl moved. *You can't scare me*, Kelly thought, transmitting the words through her glare. *Get out of the car, coward*. Finally Audra backed up and peeled out, shooting past Kelly way too fast.

Kate and Ruby, two of Kelly's most loyal followers, squealed and rushed to her side, clinging to her arms like she needed physical support. Kelly shook them off, but they continued to fuss.

"Oh, my gosh!"

"That was awful!"

"You could have died!"

Kelly ignored them, staring after the disappearing car. Blackmailer or not, Audra was asking for it. And Kelly would be only too happy to give it to her.

Chapter Twenty-two

Tom waited impatiently on the steps outside Stafford. He felt like the only student left on the grounds. The parking lot was almost empty. So where was Audra? It was not like her not to show up. She hadn't specifically promised him a ride home today, but he had come to expect it. Just like he expected her to show up in the morning and take him to school. Audra was one of the only sophomores who already had a driver's license, and the free rides were a definite perk in their friendship. In fact, the rides were feeling more and more like the *only* perk.

Annoyed, Tom took out his phone. Unlike Kelly and Alison, he didn't have a full-time chauffeur waiting for his call — he only had Audra. He would have to find a new way home. And if Audra didn't come through with his mom's file soon, he would have to —

The squeal of tires made Tom look up. A silver Audi tore up the school drive and screeched to a stop in front of Tom.

"You're late," Tom said as he climbed in.

"And you're lucky I'm here at all." Audra shot him a pointed look and immediately Tom felt awful.

"I know. I know. Sorry. I guess I'm starting to depend on you," Tom apologized, adding *too much* in his mind.

Audra smiled. "That's good." She nodded smugly. "I'm glad you know you can. I'm glad you know I'll come through for you."

Tom turned to look at Audra as she accelerated out of the parking lot, onto the road, making an oncoming car honk and hit the brakes. She'd said she would come through for him — so had she? He was afraid to ask. "Does that mean . . . Did you . . . Did you get my mom's file?"

Scrolling through tunes on the iPod player plugged into her car stereo, Audra found the song she was looking for, hit PLAY, and cranked the volume. "Sorry. Not yet," she yelled over the music.

Tom ground his teeth together. *Not yet.* He was getting tired of waiting.

Chapter Twenty-three

Zoey was in the living room tossing a book she wanted to lend Jeremy into her messenger bag when she saw Audra's car pull into the drive . . . again. *Unbelievable*, Zoey thought as she watched her brother climb out of the passenger seat. After the whole disappearing-act thing she had pretty much decided that Tom was a lost cause. If he wanted to shoot himself in the foot by picking fights with everyone who cared about him and spending all his spare time with Audra, then that was his problem. Why should Zoey care? He'd made it more than clear that he wanted nothing more to do with her, anyway. If Tom was determined to self-destruct, there was no reason for Zoey to get caught in the explosion — she would only end up getting burned.

But Alison's voice echoed in Zoey's head. "*Just because he doesn't want help doesn't mean he doesn't need it, Zo. Are you really going to let him go without trying? Are you really going to give him up to Audra?*" And deep down, Zoey knew Alison was right.

Still, it was annoying. "I can't believe you get into the car with her, Tom," Zoey yelled into the hall when she heard Tom enter. She had begun talking to him again, even though it was like trying to converse with a brick wall.

No answer.

"If Dad knew you were still getting rides from her, you wouldn't be allowed out of the house."

Still no answer.

Zoey listened to the sound of her twin shuffling around in the kitchen. She heard his cell phone ring. He picked up quickly and Zoey could tell by his hushed tone that he was talking to Audra. He obviously didn't want Zoey to hear what he was saying. Zoey shook her head in disgust and hauled herself off the couch. Audra hated to let even a second go by without having one of her claws dug into Tom. It was obsessive and crazy. Then again, so was Audra.

Everyone was talking about how Audra had tried to run Kelly down in her car after school. *Actually*, Zoey thought, *that might have been one of Audra's saner moments*. But it still proved she was a maniac. How could her brother be so blind?

Stepping into the kitchen, Zoey looked at Tom through her recently restreaked bangs and waited for him to hang up the phone.

Tom turned his back on her. "I gotta go," he mumbled into the phone. "Yeah, she's right here. Later."

"You know that girl is crazy," Zoey said. "Not like a little crazy, either. Certifiable." She was laying it on thick, she knew. But Tom had left her no choice. She was trying to get him to take the bait — to say *something*.

Tom bit. "Takes one to know one," he muttered under his breath.

"What?" Zoey asked, hoping to keep him going. "Are you comparing me to that nut job?"

"Don't call her that," Tom snarled. "You don't

know what you're talking about. She's not crazy. Her parents are psychiatrists." Tom took a step toward Zoey. "*You're* the one who's crazy. And since when is it any of your business what I do?"

"So you think it's crazy for me to care about my own brother?" Zoey shot back.

"Get off it, Zoey. You don't care about me. You're just like the rest of them — you don't care about anyone but yourself. You only hate Audra because she's smarter than you are." Tom's face was flushed.

Zoey felt her own face get hot. Her brother's words were cruel, and more important, not true. She wished for a moment that he hadn't started talking to her again. It was easier when he just gave her the silent treatment. Fighting like this just made it more obvious how much everything had changed, how far apart they had drifted since their mom died.

Taking a deep breath, Zoey lowered her voice and tried again. "Why aren't we on the same side anymore, Tom?" she asked. "Can't we look out for each other the way we used to? What happened to us?"

Tom was quiet. Instead of glaring at Zoey, he glared at the floor.

"Look." Zoey swallowed hard. She did not want to sound hysterical and was having trouble keeping the lump in her throat from leaping out of her mouth in a wail. "I just don't want to lose you . . . too," she said softly.

She saw Tom gulp. He kept his head down, and Zoey was not sure, but she thought she saw his chin quiver. Could she have broken through to him? He looked up at her and the anger was gone from his eyes.

Tom opened his mouth. But before he could speak, the doorbell rang.

Both twins turned to see Zoey's tutor, Jeremy, through the window. He was standing on the porch with his hands in his pockets. Jeremy had offered to pick Zoey up for their session today, since it was raining. They could have studied at the house, but Zoey looked for any opportunity to get out — especially if it also involved riding in the car with Jeremy, alone. Her heart thudded when she saw him. But his timing could not have been worse.

"What?" Zoey forced herself to turn back to Tom. "What were you going to say?" She put her hand on his arm and tried to draw him back into the conversation they'd been having. They were so close to actually getting somewhere she didn't want to let it go. But the moment was gone.

"Never mind." Tom jerked away. The anger returned to his voice and his eyes. He mocked Zoey as he headed for the stairs. "You have to go. Your babysitter's here."

Chapter Twenty-four

Alison held her cell phone to her ear as discreetly as possible. She was tucked into a corner of her grandmother's limo, desperate to hear a voice of reason. After three rings she hung up. Zoey wasn't answering, and she didn't exactly want to leave a message. What would she say? "Hey, Zo. Just heading to the courthouse trying not to lose my freaking mind or get caught on camera. Talk to you later." It would be easier to fill her in when it was all over — and when she was alone.

Across the car from her, Grandmother Diamond and Aunt Phoebe were sitting calmly next to each other as if they were out for a morning drive. Alison glanced over at them.

Aunt Phoebe was staring out the window, but Grandmother Diamond held Alison's gaze, then gave a small, sympathetic nod. It was a surprisingly understanding gesture, and despite all the mixed emotions Alison had been having about her grandmother, for a moment she felt almost reassured. Then the limo stopped in front of the courthouse, and the car was surrounded by flashing cameras and reporters preparing to shoot questions. The throng pressed up against the tinted glass, making Alison feel like she and her family were an exhibit at the aquarium.

"Alison." Grandmother Diamond held out an arm, indicating that Alison should take it. Fernando, the driver, opened the door and stood guard as best he could while they exited the car. Phoebe was first, then Tamara, who left her cane behind. Alison was the last to emerge, dutifully holding onto her grandmother's arm like she'd been instructed. Flanked by her granddaughter and her middle child, Tamara stood perfectly erect, waiting calmly for a path to the courthouse to clear. For a brief moment, Alison felt her own strength rise to match her grandmother's. Then a camera flashed, and her knees went weak.

Though she had seen the reporters and photographers through the windows of the limo,
their presence still hit Alison like a storm's first
blast of icy wind. Their clicking shutters and
rapid-fire questions felt like hail lashing across
her body.

"Alison, how long has it been since you've
seen your mother?"

"Mrs. Diamond, do you believe your daughter is guilty?"

"Alison, Alison, over here. Do you know
where your father is? Is it true he has a drinking
problem?"

"Tamara, we understand you and your daughter Helen are estranged. Is her arrest bringing
you back together? Tamara. Tamara!"

The Diamond women acted as though the
reporters were not even there. With their chins
perfectly raised and their mouths closed, they
walked together to the courthouse for the
highest-profile arraignment the state had seen
in decades. Alison knew they probably looked
united. But as Her Highness liked to point out,
looks were often deceiving.

Alison, for one, did not want to be at the

courthouse with her grandmother or her aunt. She didn't really want to be at the courthouse at all. But Grandmother Diamond had insisted. And Alison was in no position to refuse.

Once they entered the building, the reporters began to ease up. The judge had barred cameras from the courtroom at Helen's lawyers' request. The trial would be enough of a media circus even without them. Helen Rose was a major celebrity with a huge fan base — and plenty of detractors as well.

Alison was not sure if Helen's notoriety would help or hurt her in the end. Either way, she was glad the photographers and cameramen had to stay out, if only for her own sake.

Alison followed Aunt Phoebe and Grandmother Diamond as they took their seats behind the federal prosecutor. On the other side of the walkway, Alison recognized two of her mother's lawyers chatting near the defense table, but her mother was not yet there. Good. She hoped when her mom *did* get there she would not notice her daughter sitting on the wrong side of the courtroom . . . She hoped her mom wouldn't notice her at all.

The dark, wood-paneled room was packed. Waiting impatiently, the spectators spoke in not-so-hushed tones.

Aunt Phoebe leaned over to Alison and squeezed her hand. "It'll all be over soon," she said in her too-sweet way. "All that happens today is your mom enters her plea of guilty or not guilty," she explained as though Alison were five. "I'm sure it will all go just fine."

Alison said nothing. She used to think Aunt Phoebe was the only decent Diamond daughter. But ever since she'd overheard Phoebe and Tamara's conversation after brunch, Alison knew there were no decent Diamonds. Aunt Phoebe had taken her father from her. Even if he came back tomorrow, all sobered up, Alison would never forgive her aunt for the way it had happened. She might not forgive her father, either — for letting Phoebe talk him into it, and for not even having tried to contact Alison since he'd left. The whole thing stank.

Alison sank down in her seat, miserable at the helplessness she felt. Zoey had been pressing her to tell her mother about the papers she had stolen from Grandmother Diamond's secret vault. The way Zoey saw it, if Helen Rose ended up in prison because Alison didn't come forward, she would be subject to her grandmother's vindictiveness even more than she already was. But Alison just couldn't take that step. There was no guarantee that the documents would even help. For all she knew, her grandmother had bought off the judge. Besides, after Helen had lied to her about Tamara's visit to the jail, Alison wasn't feeling particularly warm and fuzzy toward her, either. Helen Rose was a difficult woman to trust. And as long as Alison played the good granddaughter, life with Tamara was actually pretty comfortable. The old lady was being generous with her cash, and left Alison to herself most of the time.

A door at the side of the courtroom opened and Helen entered, accompanied by two more lawyers. She was dressed in a Prada charcoal-gray skirt, a tailored jacket, and a cream-colored blouse. A lime-green scarf was tied around her neck in a stylish knot. She could have been one of the lawyers but looked even more impressively pulled together. She also appeared to be following the same game plan as her mother,

Tamara Diamond: chin up and mouth firmly closed.

The buzz of lowered voices got louder. Alison thought the whisperers must have been impressed by her mother's fresh appearance. Helen Rose looked composed, in control, and not at all guilty — more like she'd been spending the past few weeks at a spa than a jail. She seemed completely self-assured as she took her seat and gazed straight ahead, waiting for the judge to be announced. Watching her mother from behind the prosecution, Alison allowed herself to feel a tiny bit hopeful and proud.

Maybe this is going to turn out all right. Mom might not even need my help, Alison thought, *or those papers.*

Beside Alison, Grandmother Diamond sat unmoving, displaying no hint of emotion — not even when her daughter stood and announced her plea of "not guilty." Alison was dying to know what her grandmother was thinking but knew she never would.

Aunt Phoebe was not so stoic. She fidgeted in her seat and her eyes kept darting around the courtroom. Aunt Phoebe always acted skittish and nervous, even when her estranged older sister wasn't on trial, and even when she wasn't safeguarding some big secret. Still, her aunt's nervousness fanned a flame of anger inside Alison. She was pretty certain that Phoebe was *not* nervous on Helen's behalf. Not a single member of the family was on her mother's side. Alison resisted an urge to sink lower into her seat when she realized that she couldn't fully count herself as an exception.

Almost as soon as Helen sat back down, it was over. The judge was standing up and walking out. The prosecution stood, too. Alison started to lift her hand to catch her mom's attention as Helen and her lawyers stepped into the aisle, but her grandmother immediately shot out an arm to stop her. Alison suddenly wanted her mother to know she was there — supporting her. At least, sort of.

With her jaw tightly clenched, Alison craned her head to watch her mom walking out, accompanied by her counsel and a white-haired bailiff. Helen's lawyers were speaking to her in low tones. She was nodding and appeared to be listening carefully. As she passed her family, she looked purposefully over at them. She did know they were there — had probably known the whole time. Helen's eyes locked on her sister, her mother, and her daughter in turn. Her expression was unchanging, but Alison realized how she must look to her mom, seated next to the woman Helen was certain had framed her. Alison understood that was why Grandmother Diamond had wanted her there.

When Helen was gone, Tamara rose to her feet and waited for Alison to take her arm. "Don't just sit there," she snapped. Clearly their work here was done and Tamara was ready to go. Alison stood and assisted her grandmother into the busy hall.

Aunt Phoebe chattered away on Tamara's other side as they went. "That went well, all things considered, don't you think? But Helen never should have worn that color. Her skin's undertones are too yellow. She's more of a fall than a spring."

Catty to the core, Alison thought grimly. *I guess Kelly takes after both of her mothers after all.* Previously, Alison had only noticed Kelly's resemblance to selfish, calculating, and beautiful Aunt Christine. But she was no longer fooled by Aunt Phoebe.

When they got to the front exit, Alison braced herself for the reporters. She paused to put on her sunglasses, and something caught her eye. Alison did a double take.

X, the new girl at Stafford, was leaning against a wall in the courthouse, watching them.

Chapter Twenty-five

Chad looked up from his history text and checked the clock. It was only six-thirty, but he felt like he'd been studying for hours. Only he was so distracted he couldn't remember anything he'd read.

Keep this up and you'll lose your scholarship — and your girl, he told himself. Already his grades were slipping a little — and that was *with* Tom's help. And there were moments when Kelly seemed to be slipping away, too, when she seemed more interested in Tom than she was in him.

Chad rubbed his eyes and tried to focus on the paragraph swimming in front of him. Kelly wasn't really falling for Tom, was she? Chad knew that Tom had had a crush on Kelly since grade school — what guy didn't? Kelly was so incredibly captivating, and naturally flirtatious, it was impossible not to adore her. She made everyone she paid the slightest bit of attention to feel like the luckiest person in the world.

But Tom had been flirting with Kelly a little too much lately, and a little too publicly. And meanwhile, Tom seemed to have next to no time for Chad. The only person he had the time of day for was Audra.

Chad opened his laptop — a hand-me-down Dell from his dad's work — and clicked on his mail icon. He hit NEW MESSAGE and started to type. He wouldn't tell Tom he was upset about the flirting, he would just tell him he wanted to talk . . . again. Chad owed his best friend at least one more chance.

Chapter Twenty-six

"Oh, you eat just like a bird!" Deirdre chirped, hanging over Tom's shoulder. Tom hunched lower over his dinner plate and forced in another bite. His new stepmother was making him lose what was left of his appetite — which was not exactly hearty to begin with. Lately just being in his house made him feel sick. At least his father wasn't around much. The DA had slipped right back into his old routine of work, work, work, and no time for his family. Whether his dad was trying to avoid his short-tempered son or his vapid new bride, Tom didn't know. Either way, he was grateful for his father's absence.

"You've got to eat more, honey, or people will think I'm a bad mommy." Deirdre massaged Tom's shoulders, and his muscles tightened. Her long, painted fingernails snagged on his wool sweater. That did it. He pushed his plate away and stood up from the table, shrugging off her awful touch.

"Leave me alone," he growled. "You are *not* my mother."

Deirdre gasped, her eyes widening, just as the front door opened and DA Ramirez walked into the kitchen and set his briefcase on the counter. Tom followed him with his eyes, daring his father to look his way, to speak to him. But his old man didn't even acknowledge Tom's presence in the room. He sat at the table with his newspaper while Deirdre fluttered around him, pouring his wine and getting his plate from the oven.

Tom stood by his chair, waiting, almost *craving* a confrontation. The lectures and blowups didn't faze him anymore — in fact, he found them almost satisfying. All of his father's strong-arming just demonstrated the DA's weakness.

He could yell and threaten all he wanted, but he couldn't touch Tom.

Actually, since the blowup after his crazy road trip with Audra, the DA had barely acknowledged him. Maybe Tom's father had finally realized how useless barking orders was. He certainly hadn't attempted anything resembling a *conversation* with his son. Of course, conversation required give-and-take. His father was only ever good at dishing it out.

Tom continued to stare at his father, and his father continued to ignore him. Before the wedding, the DA would not have stood for this. He would have yelled at Tom to go do something useful, like study. It occurred to Tom that calling his dad on his involvement in his mother's "accident" had given him a small advantage. For the first time, DA Daddy was trying to stay off of *Tom's* radar and not the other way around. Mr. Ramirez was the one on the defensive — probably hoping Tom would not bring up the subject of his mother again, ever. And in Tom's mind, his father's avoidance only further proved his guilt.

Without clearing his plate, Tom turned and stalked away from the dinner table. He took the stairs to his bedroom two at a time, stepped inside, and slammed his door, confident that his dad wouldn't yell about it. Not anymore.

Chapter Twenty-seven

Alone at last, Tom had barely begun to decompress when his phone rang. Audra. Of course. The girl was always right there, whether he needed her or not. *Not now,* Tom thought.

Ignoring the ring, Tom sat down at his desk and cracked a book. A second later, his phone beeped. He had a text message. Audra again. He was sure before he even looked.

I NO U R HOME, he read.

Was she sitting outside again? Tom dropped to his knees and crawled over to the window to look out. Sure enough, the TT was there, parked across the street. He couldn't see her through the tinted windows, but he could just picture her sitting inside with her feet up on the dash, texting away on her phone.

Tom leaned against the wall and texted back. Maybe she had finally brought him his mother's file. She had been sort of teasing him with it — promising he could see it and then always "forgetting" to bring it. Maybe tonight she had come through at last.

DO U HAVE THE FILE? he asked.

His heart raced at the thought. He missed his mom so much. He would do anything to feel like she was around again — like she was there for him — even if it was something as questionable as reading her psychiatrist's notes.

NO, the answer came back.

Tom pounded his fist on the floor. He was getting really fed up with Audra's lurking around and dangling information but never delivering it. She had definitely made a nice little escape hatch for him in the last couple of weeks. But her neediness was growing and her usefulness was almost at an end. She was getting annoying.

A new message arrived: IS THAT ALL U WANT ME 4?

Tom had an urge to throw his phone across

the room. *Actually, Audra, I don't want you at all.* Their relationship had lost its luster. He was fed up. Maybe Zoey was right about Audra. Not that that would be any consolation.

STOP STALKING ME. U R CRA-Z, he typed impulsively.

Ten seconds later he had a reply: NOT AS CRA-Z AS U.

As he read the message, Tom knew Audra was right, which made him madder. *Why is the only person who seems to get me such a weirdo?* he wondered with a groan. He closed his eyes, not wanting to deal with this now. But Audra was nothing if not relentless.

I KNOW U BETTER THAN U KNOW YRSELF. U NEED ME, he read a moment later.

Tom slid down the wall the rest of the way so he was lying on the floor looking up at the ceiling. He was as low as he could go. *I do need her,* Tom thought. *I need her because she understands. Problem is, I don't want her.*

Then a new thought set Tom's fingers in motion. He scrolled down his list of contacts, stopping at K. *Audra understands because I talk to her. Because I let her in. Kelly could understand. . . . She* would *understand. If I could just get close enough.*

Remembering the way Kelly had wiped his chin at lunch the day before and the way she had been looking at him, Tom fanned the little spark of hope igniting within him. Maybe Kelly was just waiting for him to make a move. She was definitely the kind of girl who appreciated being chased. And there was no denying the way she was flirting with him lately — right in front of Chad, too.

Chad. Just the idea of him burned Tom up. He used to think he would never stoop so low as to make a play for his best friend's girl. But Chad hardly felt like a friend anymore. And if he wasn't being good enough to Kelly to hold on to her, well, that was *his* problem. Chad got *everything* handed to him *all* the time. He slipped from girl-friend to girlfriend without even trying. And he got a free ride at school — not to mention the answers to all of his homework, compliments of Tom. How come Tom had to work hard while Chad got to coast? It was not fair.

Tom was finished standing loyally by Chad and carrying his friend's deadweight. It was time for Tom to go after what he so desperately wanted. It was time for things to go *his* way for a change — with Kelly Reeves at his side.

If only.

That would never happen for him.

Would it?

Tom took a deep breath. He had to know. With nothing left to lose, he pushed SEND and stared at the words on his phone screen.

DIALING KELLY REEVES.

Chapter Twenty-eight

Kelly sat up on her king-sized bed, dropped the TV remote, and grabbed her phone the second it rang. Tom.

Well, well. Kelly hit a button. Tom never called her. Maybe Chad was with him and had lost his phone.

"Hey, Tom. What's up?" Kelly asked, reclining against her satin pillows and turning back to the huge, flat-screen TV. She was only half listening to Tom babble when something made her seriously stop and hit MUTE on the remote.

"What?"

"I said, he doesn't deserve you. He doesn't

appreciate you. Not the way I would. Not the way I do. If you'll just give me a chance, I —"

"Hang on a sec, Tom." Kelly sat up, giving the conversation her full attention. If Tom was actually making a play for her — well, that was rich! The poor boy was around the bend. A devilish smile spread across Kelly's face. This could get *very* interesting. The possibilities were simply endless.

Kelly kept Tom waiting as she quickly ran through it all in her head. Tom's offer was tempting. Audra would never recover if Kelly worked this right. And Kelly didn't feel particularly attached to Chad — she could consider ditching him. Except then Chad might go running back to Alison. There was no way she could have that. She needed to hold on to her current boyfriend a little longer. But that didn't mean she couldn't still get something out of this situation. She might as well at least let Tom finish what he had to say.

"Sorry, Tom. I'm back. What were you saying?" Kelly cooed.

Tom cleared his throat and began again.

He sounded flustered, almost breathless. "I hope you don't think I'm crazy. I just had to tell you."

Kelly had had all the time she needed to weigh her options, and she decided she wanted to keep them wide open. Why choose when she could have it all?

"I'm so flattered, Tom," she said soothingly. "I think the world of you. But the timing is all wrong. I can't leave Chad now, not with everything that's going on with Will."

Kelly paused, waiting to see what Tom would say. Bringing up Chad's little brother was risky, but she was pretty sure Tom knew all about that secret. She hoped so. Will was the best excuse she had. And Kelly loved how sweet and thoughtful it made her seem.

Tom was beginning to sound desperate. "Still, he doesn't deserve you. He really doesn't."

And you do? Kelly was growing bored.

"He has no idea what he's got."

Well, that's true. Kelly flipped through a few channels while letting Tom spin himself out. Nothing was on. Then her phone beeped.

"Tom? I have another call. Talk to you later, okay?" Kelly switched over. "Chad!" Nice timing.

"Hi, Kelly. Just thinking about you."

"That's funny." Kelly switched off the TV. "Tom and I were just talking about you."

"Tom?" Chad's voice was tight. "You're with Tom?"

"No," Kelly said. "He just called."

"What'd he want?" Chad demanded.

"Oh . . ." Kelly tried to keep her tone casual. "Actually, me," she said with a giggle. The silence on the other end of the phone told her she was the only one who was amused. "It was no big deal. He just finally confessed that crush he's had on me for years . . . and told me what an ungrateful boyfriend I have."

Chad was silent.

Kelly sat back, feeling thoroughly satisfied. There was nothing like a bit of healthy competition to make a guy sit up and take notice.

"Ungrateful? He's the one who's ungrateful!" Chad finally managed to choke out. Kelly could just picture him fuming. His ears always turned adorably red at the tips when he was mad.

"Oh, don't be upset. I'm sure he was joking! You know Tom. He's hilarious when he gets going."

"Yeah, I know Tom. He's a real riot. Hysterical." Chad's voice was deadpan. He was almost never sarcastic. Kelly could tell he was really mad.

This was going to make even more fireworks than Kelly had dreamed. And Chad had really hit the nail on the head when he used the word *hysterical*. Tom had sounded even nuttier than his pyro sister, or hit-and-run queen Audra — but Chad didn't need to know that.

Glancing at the clock, Kelly swung her legs over the edge of the bed. "Hey, sweetie, I've got to go," she announced. Chad started to interrupt, but she ignored him. "See you tomorrow!"

She snapped her phone shut and laughed out loud. That was the best unplanned chain of events to come her way in a long time. But now it was time to prepare for the next *planned* affair — she'd invited herself to dinner at Grandmother Diamond's estate. *Surprise, Alison!*

Chapter Twenty-nine

Alison closed her book and rolled over on her bed. It was almost time for dinner, time to play the dutiful granddaughter through another formal meal with Tamara. Just the thought of it made Alison feel fidgety. Ever since the arraignment, she and her grandmother had not spent much time together, but whenever they were together Tamara acted as though everything were perfectly normal. If anything, she had been nicer than usual. But sitting through meals, making pleasant small-talk with her grandmother while her mother rotted in jail was making Alison feel more and more like a traitor. Of course, her mom had just *lied* to her. But

Grandmother Diamond was no saint . . . and Alison was still caught in the middle. The whole thing made her stomach turn.

I wonder if I can just skip it, Alison mused. She could tell one of the servants she had a sore throat and ask to have her meal sent to her room. Grandmother Diamond probably wouldn't even check on her — Her Highness detested germs. Now that sounded like a plan.

Alison slipped off the carved canopy bed. She had just enough time to make her excuses before Francesca rang the bell to alert the household that the evening meal was ready to be served.

Just as she reached the door, a knock on the other side sent Alison scurrying back to her bed. She wasn't sure who was out in the hall, but she certainly hoped it was one of the servants and not her grandmother. Of course, Grandmother Diamond never knocked — because, she said, in her house there were no secrets. Alison found that laughable. Who was she kidding? But just in case it was the lady of the mansion, Alison wanted to make sure she looked like she was coming down with something.

"Come in," Alison called out, making her

voice as raspy as possible and pulling her goose-down duvet over her legs.

The door opened and Kelly stepped inside. "Well, don't you look cozy," she said sweetly, looking around like she was inspecting the joint.

Suddenly Alison started to feel sick for real. How long had Kelly been at the estate? Her cousin was showing up way too often. She was taking every opportunity she could find to kiss up to Grandmother Diamond and make sure Alison's life was acceptably miserable. And the worst part was, it was working.

"Not bad . . . for a prison cell." Kelly finished her appraisal of the room and sat down on Alison's bed without being asked. Alison felt totally trapped under her blanket and her cous-in's evil eye.

"Do you want something?" Alison asked, irritated.

"Ooh, testy." Kelly's green eyes flashed. "Better watch yourself, Al. I came in because of something *you* want." Kelly pulled a postcard out of her Balenciaga metallic tote bag and waved it in the air.

"I don't want that," Alison snapped, not caring what it was. She just wanted Kelly to leave. She was getting hot under her covers, fully dressed. But it would be weird to climb out now and let Kelly see that she'd jumped into bed with her shoes on.

"Well, it's addressed to you." Kelly tossed the postcard on the bed. It landed facedown. The beautiful beach scene on the front looked tranquil and calm. Alison felt anything but.

Alison reached for the card cautiously. She knew better than to think Kelly was doing her some sort of favor. As far as she was concerned, the card was a snake that might bite.

Slowly Alison turned the card over. Her eyes widened. It was from her dad! Emotions collided inside Alison. Relief that her dad had finally contacted her, anger that he was living it up in some tropical resort while she was still trapped here, and nervousness at what it all meant. She quickly scanned the stamp and postmark. The card was sent from Belize, a small country in Central America.

Her dad had not written much. But Alison didn't read it yet. She could feel Kelly's eyes on her, watching for her reaction. She wanted to be alone. Whatever the card said, Kelly must have already read it. "Where did you —"

"I found it on the table in the foyer, and I thought I should give it to you before someone threw it away," Kelly explained. Alison's head shot up. There was no malice in her cousin's voice. She actually sounded sincere.

For about half a second Alison felt like Kelly might really have brought her the card to be nice. There was a time when the two of them had stood together against the crazy machinations of their shared family. It was only a couple of months ago that Kelly and Alison had ditched Sunday brunch and all the crazy Diamonds to go shopping. Kelly came up with a great lie about being on the committee for some charitable event. They had even gotten a sizable "donation" from their grandmother (which they used to buy shoes). *That was then. This is now*, she thought, reminding herself just whom she was talking to.

Standing up, Kelly crossed to the door. "You deserve to know where he is at least," she said softly, before opening the door.

Alison blinked rapidly, glad that Kelly was headed out. Kelly being nice to her was even harder to take than Kelly being mean. "Thanks," she whispered before the door closed.

Throwing off the covers, Alison paced, reading her father's words at last.

Dear Alison,

I know you must be mad. I've sent so many letters and have heard nothing from you.

The good news is I feel like I am getting better. I wish I could be there for you and your mom now. Please know I will be soon. Until then, it's up to you. You hold the key.

Love,

Dad

There was no return address, but her father clearly believed Alison already knew how to contact him. And it sounded like he had written to her several times before. The loss of those letters hit Alison deep in her gut. That was probably why Kelly had brought her this postcard, she realized — to make sure Alison knew that there had been others she would never get to read. Others that Kelly or Grandmother Diamond had probably already destroyed.

Alison read the card again, memorizing every word, every letter. What was "up to her"? Those last two sentences made her feel more helpless and frustrated than ever. True, she held the key — the small, silver key her father had left her — but she still had no idea what to do with it.

Downstairs the dinner bell rang. With Kelly here, Alison knew she could not play sick. Her cousin had just done something sort of nice, which could only mean she was moving in for the kill. For a split-second Alison wondered if Kelly might have even faked the postcard, but she knew the handwriting was her dad's. And she was pretty certain that Kelly didn't know about the key. At any rate, Alison was going to have to sit through the meal to keep an eye on her cousin.

She shoved the postcard under her mattress, glanced in the mirror, and gave her hair a quick fix. As Alison made her way down the stairs she donned her poker face. Dinner was served. Game on.

Chapter Thirty

Zoey kicked happily at the first few fallen leaves on the sidewalk as she walked home from Hardwired. She and Jeremy had spent two hours together and not a second of it had been wasted on schoolwork. Zoey just loved the fact that her father insisted on — and paid for — their twice-a-week chatfests. To Zoey the tutoring sessions felt much more like dates. She and Jeremy got to hole up at a cozy table for two, sip coffees, make jokes, and flick brownie crumbs at each other, all on Daddy's dime. Today had been especially fabulous because that new girl, X, had come into the café right when Jeremy was picking a stray bit of chocolate out of Zoey's hair.

Zoey grinned remembering the moment. It must have looked like the two of them were together, and Zoey felt a secret thrill at the thought of *that* getting spread around school instead of the usual rumors about why she had been kicked out of so many boarding schools. But who knew if X was a gossip spreader? If she thought about it, Zoey didn't think X seemed the type. She was too cool for gossip. She was practically too cool for Stafford.

Zoey realized that the chances of Jeremy wanting to be more than friends were slim. But there was no doubt in her mind that he didn't show up to tutor her for the money. He really seemed to care about her. And she cared about him, too. After Alison, he was the person she trusted the most in all of Silver Spring.

Yeah, Zoey felt good. Really good. *And nothing*, she thought, taking a deep breath of the cool evening air, *is going to spoil my mood*. Then she spotted the nasty blemish parked in her otherwise perfectly manicured neighborhood. The silver stalker-mobile was sitting across the street from her house, again. And surely Audra was holed up inside, watching every movement of the Ramirez family through her tinted windows.

Zoey felt a flash of anger. She was sick of being spied on in her own house! Audra was always lurking — Zoey'd had to keep her bedroom shades down for weeks.

Enough was enough. Moving quickly, Zoey marched up to the driver's-side window and rapped on it, hard.

Audra lowered it a crack, but did not look up.

"Leave now or I am calling the cops," Zoey threatened. Really, she had no intention of involving the police. That would only get her dad involved and make Tom mad and . . . ew. But Audra didn't have to know the threat was empty.

"It's a public street," Audra said, still not making eye contact — her gaze was fixed on Tom's window.

"Actually, it's a private community," Zoey corrected her. "And if you know what's good for you, you'll leave before I get my dad to file a restraining order."

"You wouldn't," Audra said, finally whipping her head around to glare at Zoey.

"Try me," Zoey bluffed.

Apparently — amazingly — that was enough.

Audra rolled her eyes. "I was just leaving." She smiled fakely at Zoey before starting the car and throwing it into gear.

Zoey stood in the middle of the street watching the TT disappear from sight. As the leaves settled back around her, Zoey seethed. If only that girl would just keep on driving.

Chapter Thirty-one

Chad's head pounded. He could feel the blood coursing through his veins so hard, his entire body was throbbing. Sleep was impossible.

The red glowing numbers on his digital clock were the only light in the room. Chad stared at them, unblinking. 2:38.

"Forget it!" Chad threw off his blankets and turned on a light. He paced his small room, kicking aside his gym bag. It was taking all the self-control he had not to walk the three miles to Tom's house right that minute and bang down the door. Chad wanted to confront his former best friend face-to-face. He wanted to look Tom in the eye when he dared him to deny trying to steal his girlfriend out from under him. And the sooner, the better.

Chad put both hands on his head and pushed in, trying to relieve the pressure inside. When Kelly had told him about Tom's call, he'd gone ballistic. She had played it off like it was some kind of joke — and she was so good-hearted, she probably actually believed that — but Chad was no idiot. He knew the difference between a prank and a betrayal.

It was no secret that Tom had a crush on Kelly. He'd been in love with her forever. But so were lots of guys — lots of guys who weren't Chad's best friend. There was a code of conduct with friends, and you didn't break it. Even before this, Tom had been crossing the line, flirting with Kelly in front of him. Humiliating him.

Sure, Chad had seen how Kelly flirted back and encouraged Tom a little. But Kelly couldn't help it. She was too sweet and considerate to tell Tom to cut it out — that would just make him feel lame. Flirting was second nature to her. *It's just how she is,* Chad thought. *She probably doesn't even realize she's doing it.* Tom was definitely to blame. His blatant play for Kelly had just proved it. And the fact that Kelly had told Chad all about it proved that he could trust her.

Chad slumped into the bathroom and tugged on the top of a bottle of pain relievers. He had been taking the orange pills a lot lately, for his head. Except they never helped. The top came off and pills toppled out all over the sink, slipping down the drain and bouncing off the counter.

"Great." Chad dropped to his knees to gather the tablets that had fallen on the floor. He swallowed four, then went back to his room. 2:41. Only five hours until his friendship with Tom would be officially down the drain, too, and Chad could finally stop feeling like a fool.

Chad was just climbing back into bed when his phone rang, making him jump. He picked it up and glanced at the caller ID. Dustin, his older brother. Great. Like Chad needed one more problem to deal with.

"It's three o'clock in the morning," he complained in lieu of hello.

"Touchy, touchy," Dustin replied with a laugh. "Who are you, Dad? Besides, I can tell you weren't even asleep. You picked up too fast."

"Right," Chad mumbled, wishing his father had remembered to take his phone away at nine like he usually did. Right now he didn't want to get into it with his older brother. Since Dustin had gotten kicked out of the house a few weeks ago, he only ever called to ask for money. But, Chad suddenly realized, he hadn't heard from Dustin in a while — a trend he didn't want to upset.

"Anyway, I just wanted to call and see how you're doing," Dustin said. "You know, how things are going in Chad's world."

"Fine, they're fine," Chad lied, feeling annoyed. Since when did Dustin care about his life?

"Hey, don't take it out on me," Dustin said, picking up on Chad's angry tone. "I didn't do anything."

Maybe not lately, Chad thought. "I said I'm fine," Chad repeated. But Dustin was clearly intent on having a chat. The quickest way to get rid of him would be to talk to him. "Mom and Dad have cooled off a little, and Will is doing okay at school. And Kelly is better than ever."

There was a pause on the other end of the

line. "Right, Kelly," Dustin repeated. "I thought girls were supposed to be the gold diggers, not guys. But I guess she's using you, too, in her own way."

"Hey, I am not with her for her money," Chad said disgustedly. Only Dustin, who was worse with money than he was with rules, would think that. What right did he have to make comments about him and Kelly, anyway? Dustin didn't know the first thing about Chad's girlfriend or their relationship.

Unbelievable, Chad thought. It was so typical for Dustin to decide to play the older brother now, after he'd set such a great example that their father had kicked him out of the house.

"Just don't say I didn't warn you, little bro," Dustin said lightly. Everything was always a joke to him — even Chad's life.

"Whatever, Dustin," Chad replied. "Are you done dispensing advice yet? I'd like to go to sleep sometime tonight." Without waiting for an answer, he held down the END button until the power blinked off. If Dustin had anything else to say to Chad, Chad didn't want to hear it.

Chapter Thirty-two

The next day at school dragged on and on while Chad bided his time. He wanted to confront Tom alone, on his own. He wanted Tom to know that he was seriously hurt, and he didn't want an audience. This was not some lunchroom drama. This was *real*.

Finally, during PE, Chad caught Tom in the hall by himself. He took three running steps and shoved Tom's frame into the lockers — hard. The noise of the impact on the metal echoed in the hall. "What's up, buddy?" Chad spat, getting up in Tom's face. "Made a move on your best friend's girl lately?"

Tom regained his balance and stood his full

height. He had at least two inches and twenty pounds on Chad, but Chad had surprise on his side. And anger. He watched as Tom's expression changed from confusion to disgust. "She told you?" he asked.

"Told me you were a double-crossing low-life scum?" Chad pushed in even closer. "Nah. I figured that out on my own." Chad was so angry, he was seeing spots. He took a shallow breath. "Of course she told me!" he yelled. "She's my girlfriend! And you, you're supposed to be my best friend!"

Tom shoved Chad away, hard, then took two steps and shoved him again.

Chad stumbled dizzily and fell backward, hitting his head on the lockers that lined the other side of the hall. The impact was like being hit with a sledgehammer, and he felt himself slipping to the floor. It was a long way down.

"At least I'm not a liar and a cheat," Tom snarled.

Chapter Thirty-three

Tom watched Chad stagger to his feet. His ex-best friend looked stung. Dazed, too. It certainly took him a long time to stand up. He was practically finished. But Tom wasn't. In fact, he was just getting started. Chad wouldn't be getting a free pass this time around.

"You're pathetic," Tom growled, stepping closer. "You act like you think you're some kind of saint. You get everything handed to you on a silver platter and you *still* can't hack it!" Tom wasn't about to take any flak from Chad about calling Kelly, and he certainly wasn't sorry he'd done it. Chad had been using Tom for too long to start acting all self-righteous now.

Chad took a step back, groping for support and finding it on the bank of lockers. Tom had barely even touched him yet, but already he looked down for the count. Tom kept on, moving closer. Chad had nowhere to run and no one to hide behind. "I'm sick of being treated like your slave boy," he shouted in Chad's face. "I'm tired of cheating for you and doing your lousy homework so you can be with Kelly and protect your precious scholarship. I'm sick of your whining. If you can't cut it at Stafford, you shouldn't even be here. You're scum, Chad. You're a poseur and a loser — and a lousy friend."

Laying into Chad like this felt great. Tom should have done it a long time ago. All of the anger pent up inside him — rage at his dad, his sister, Audra, his out-of-control life — came roaring out of him.

"Your free ride is over, Chad." Crossing his arms over his chest, Tom waited to see what Chad would do next.

Chad shakily pushed himself off the wall of lockers and finally found his tongue. "You think . . ." He stopped and steadied himself. "You think helping me with my homework gives you the right to help yourself to my girlfriend? Your work isn't even that good," he gasped. "The last 'help' you gave me got me an F."

Tom smiled cruelly, remembering the wrong answers he'd given Chad. He had almost forgotten. He was glad Chad reminded him. The loser deserved that F, no question.

Over Chad's shoulder, a familiar golden glint caught Tom's eye. Tom didn't have to look twice to know Kelly had rounded the corner. She must have heard the commotion and come to check out the action. The show was nearly over — Kelly was just in time for the grand finale.

"You were using me, Chad, and you know it," Tom hissed. "Just like you're using Kelly. She's just another rung up on the social ladder for you. You never really cared about her — not like I did. Not like I *do*." Tom looked past Chad and locked eyes with Kelly. He wanted to see her reaction. Her green eyes looked back at him evenly, but they gave away nothing.

Behind Kelly a second pair of eyes was watching, framed by glasses. Audra. Of course she was there. She was everywhere Tom was.

Tom turned back to Chad, glaring, daring

him to make another move. Chad looked weirdly dazed, but also like he wanted to take a swing at him. Tom hoped he would. He'd welcome the chance to pummel his former friend. But Chad would lose that fight in a huge way and he knew it. Tom had the upper hand, and not just physically.

Tom saw fear flicker in Chad's eyes and smirked. The reality of his position had finally dawned on him. Tom was well aware that Chad didn't want anyone to know about his scholarship. His reputation was on the line, as was his enrollment. Getting caught cheating *or* fighting could get Chad expelled. His whole academic career was hanging in the balance — and Tom was holding the strings.

Of course Tom was involved in the cheating, and the fighting, too. But in the long run he was safe. He and Chad both knew that Tom Ramirez's position at Stafford was assured. The academy would never risk losing DA Ramirez's money or political clout by kicking out his son.

"I'm telling the dean everything," Tom said in a low voice. "Our friendship is over. And so are you."

Chapter Thirty-four

Zoey unlocked the bathroom stall and stepped up to the sink to wash her hands. She was just reaching for a towel when Ruby, one of Kelly's lackeys, turned away from her own reflection to give Zoey a once-over. "Don't you think you should be looking for your brother?" she asked, smoothing pale pink gloss across her lips.

Zoey stared at her blankly. "Tom?"

"None other. He just freaked out at Chad in the hall."

"What?" Zoey asked. A knot was quickly forming in the pit of her stomach.

"Well . . ." Ruby lit up at the opportunity to spread a little gossip. She must have been desperate if she was talking to Zoey. Either that or the gossip was just too hot not to spill. "Apparently Chad and Tom were going at it, big-time. Your brother totally flipped out at him for, like, no reason, and then took off in a hurry. You didn't hear?" she added, twisting the lip-gloss tube closed. "It's kinda funny, actually." She waved the lip gloss in the air. "I always thought *you* were the crazy one. And then it's Tom who goes off the deep —"

"Thanks," Zoey snarled as she pushed past the Kelly clone. She didn't wait to hear more. She had to get to Tom immediately.

Stay calm, she told herself as she slammed out of the bathroom and raced through the Stafford halls. *You'll find him.* But she wasn't so sure. This was the moment Zoey had been waiting for — and dreading. After teetering on the edge for weeks, Tom had finally gone over. Zoey desperately wanted to catch him. Or at the very least, be there to help him pick up the pieces after he crashed.

Except that she had no idea where her brother was, where he'd disappeared to after the fight.

Zoey checked the gym. Not there. She

checked the class he was supposed to be in. No sign. Where the heck was he?

I can help him, Zoey thought. *I can save him. I have to.* She could not let Tom sink so far down that he never resurfaced. Not like their mom.

Her heart thumping in her chest, Zoey rounded a corner by Tom's locker. But the hall was empty. She ran back the way she came, toward the main exit. Bursting outside, Zoey squinted into the slanted light and spotted a silver Audi TT heading off campus.

Thank goodness, Zoey thought. She'd found him. Now if she could just get him out of Audra's clutches . . .

Panting, Zoey threw herself in front of the car. It screeched to a halt and Zoey yanked open the passenger door. The passenger seat was empty. Audra was alone.

"Get in," Audra ordered, expressionless.

"Where's Tom?" Zoey demanded. If anyone knew where he was, it would be Audra.

"I'll take you to him," Audra promised.

Zoey didn't hesitate. Her heart pounding, she climbed inside.

Chapter Thirty-five

Chad remained in the hall, leaning against a locker, his head spinning. Tom was gone, thank goodness. He didn't have to defend himself anymore. Not that he could, anyway. He was feeling weak. And even on Chad's best day, Tom was bigger, stronger. And, Chad had to admit, at least a little bit right.

Don't think about that now, Chad told himself. *You need to pull it together, get to class.* But Chad couldn't seem to focus. Or move very fast. His head was killing him where it had hit the locker.

My life here is over, Chad thought, closing his eyes. *And my best friend is now my enemy.*

The bell rang. The noise was earsplitting. Throngs of students filled the hall. Chad opened his eyes and scanned the blurry crowd for Kelly. He thought he'd caught a glimpse of her during the fight, but then she'd disappeared, just like Tom. Why hadn't she come to his aid? He suddenly pictured her face in the hall, smiling . . . at Tom. That couldn't be right, could it? A new thought brought a bitter taste into his mouth. Maybe Tom and Kelly had disappeared together.

He put his hands on his pounding head and squeezed his eyes shut again. He desperately wanted the pounding to go away, but it was only getting worse. . . .

Chad opened his eyes. The halls had emptied. Black spots swam in front of him — and something else, too. A person. Kelly?

Chad squinted. No, it wasn't Kelly. This person had darker hair and a softer voice. It was Alison.

Chad reached out his hands to her, relieved to see a friend. And not just any friend, either. Alison. The girl he should never have broken up with.

Feelings of gratefulness flooded over him. Alison always managed to be there for him when he needed her most. "Alison, I . . ." Chad struggled to form words. His mouth wasn't working well. He wanted to apologize, to explain, to erase the last couple of months from existence. He understood now. He knew what it felt like to be abandoned and betrayed by the people closest to you — how much it hurt. How terribly he and Kelly had treated her. She hadn't deserved that. Nobody did, but especially not Alison. And after everything he had done to her, here she was, coming over to see if *he* was okay.

"I've been such an idiot," Chad whispered hoarsely. He felt overwhelmingly weak, but he had to get this out right now, before it was too late.

"It'll be okay," Alison told him, taking his arm reassuringly and helping him stand upright.

"I know." Chad shook his head, trying to clear the spots still dancing in front of him. "Alison, I'm so sorry." Finally his long-overdue apology was out.

"It's —" Alison started to say.

Chad put a shaky finger to her lips. There was something else he wanted to tell her — something he needed to say . . . something he finally realized was true.

"I still love you," he murmured.

Chapter Thirty-six

Alison stared at Chad's face, searching it. She felt as though the floor had just fallen out from under her. She'd heard the words he'd just spoken but had no idea what to do with them. He *still* loved her? He still *loved* her?

In her heart she wanted to believe that it was true he was sorry, that he was still a decent person, that he still cared about her, and that Kelly had been the one behind everything. It would feel really good to know she hadn't been completely wrong about him.

"Alison?" Chad whispered, leaning forward and looking into her eyes. "Did you hear what I said?"

Alison nodded and closed her eyes. Of course she did. Those were the words she'd longed to hear so many times. Words she'd hoped against hope that she would hear again from this boy's lips. She still cared about him . . . a lot. But she'd spent the last couple of months trying to get over him, trying to move on. She'd thought at last that she finally had.

Looking up into Chad's big brown eyes, all of Alison's old feelings — feelings she'd tried to bury — were flooding back. And they were crashing down on her with the strength of a tidal wave.

She had not been expecting this.

Alison bit her lip. What could she say to him? That he'd hurt her so badly she'd wanted to crawl under a rock and die? That the past few months had been really hard without him? "Chad, I . . ."

Alison trailed off. Chad's eyes suddenly looked very far away. "Chad?" Alison repeated.

Chad opened his mouth to speak. Then, in an instant, his legs crumpled under him.

"Chad!" Alison screamed as he fell into her, his weight nearly knocking them both to the floor. She struggled to lay him gently down on the tile. She kneeled over him, looking into his eyes. They were open but completely blank. Chad was unconscious.

"Call 911!" Alison shouted to the first person she saw.

"Is that really necessary?" Kelly asked, rolling her eyes as she sauntered closer. "He just fainted, right?"

"*Now!*" Alison ordered. She looked down and saw blood begin to trickle out of Chad's nose. In no time at all, the thin stream turned into a river of crimson. Alison pulled Chad's head onto her lap, trying to stop the flow, ignoring the fact that her clothes were getting covered in blood.

Kelly cringed. Then, slowly, she pulled her phone out of her bag and dialed the number.

Alison grabbed one of Chad's hands. "Hold on," she whispered as her eyes welled with tears. "Just hold on."

Chapter Thirty-seven

Kelly stared at Chad's unmoving body as his blood pooled onto the floor. Gross. It was *really* too bad he'd decided to pass out at that precise moment, because she'd been ready to dump him right then and there.

Standing just around the corner, she'd heard his pathetic professions of love. It was absolutely sickening. Kelly had been about to cut him loose when Alison had screamed. Kelly had turned the corner just in time to watch her boyfriend crumple into her cousin's Ya-Ya clad arms. These two wimps deserved each other — not that Kelly would allow them to be together again . . . ever.

Kelly's green eyes coolly took it all in as the paramedics rushed down the hall. Within seconds they were all over Chad, shooing Alison out of the way.

"We've got a pulse," one of them shouted, laying Chad's limp wrist back down on the tile.

"And he's breathing," another called, lifting his ear from Chad's mouth. "It's shallow, but consistent." He checked Chad's eyes, pulling back the lids and shining a penlight into them, while another one put an oxygen mask over his face.

Kelly began to feel a little more interested and excited — this was just like TV.

One of the paramedics squatted down next to Alison on the floor, asking questions. "You were with him when he collapsed?"

"Yes," Alison replied. "We were standing right here talking," she said, sniffling. "And all of a sudden he had this look on his face, like he knew something was wrong. Then his eyes went blank and he collapsed."

Kelly stepped forward. "Oh, Alison, you must feel terrible," she said. "Upsetting him like that."

"I didn't upset him!" Alison insisted. "We were just . . ."

The paramedic put his hand on Alison's arm. "Nothing you said could have caused this boy to black out," he said reassuringly as he turned back to Chad.

"Or at least you can tell yourself that," Kelly added slyly.

Alison tried to ignore her, but Kelly could tell she was making her point. As a crowd of students and teachers gathered around, Alison just sat there on the floor looking totally dazed and sad, as if Chad were *her* boyfriend. Except, Kelly remembered with a glimmer of triumph, he wasn't.

"Oh, Chad!" she suddenly wailed, throwing herself at his feet. "Is he going to be okay? Chad, wake up! Come back!"

Alison stared at Kelly, her eyes growing wider. She was clearly appalled by Kelly's performance. But the rest of her audience was eating it up. Kelly was not one to disappoint a crowd.

But even as the paramedics worked to revive him, Chad remained limp as wet toast. Kelly allowed the school nurse to pull her off him and murmur words of comfort.

"He's not coming around," the head paramedic barked. "Let's get him to the ambulance, pronto. This boy is in a coma."

Chapter Thirty-eight

Audra stepped on the gas and careened around a curve. Out of the corner of her eye, she saw Zoey tighten her grip on the seat. Her other hand clutched her seat belt so tightly that her knuckles were white. Audra smirked. If Zoey thought this was dangerous, wait until they got to their destination.

"You said you were taking me to Tom," Zoey piped up. Audra could tell she was trying to sound stern, but her voice shook slightly. *What a loser.* Audra knew she had the advantage already, and they hadn't even gotten out of the car yet. Adrenaline surged through her as she pressed harder on the gas. They were almost at the bridge.

"There's no way he got this far out of town," Zoey continued. "Pull over right now. I want out."

And that's exactly what you'll be getting, Audra thought. She had to help Tom get free of the things that were ruining his life, starting with his sister. Then he would see. Then he would love her. He'd *have* to love her.

Audra slammed on the brakes and sent the car spinning in a 180. The TT shuddered to a stop in the middle of a suspension bridge, the front end just inches from the guardrail. The bridge spanned a rushing white river far below. A quarter mile downstream, the river emptied into a lake Zoey should know well. Her brother certainly did.

"Look familiar?" Audra asked, raising an eyebrow. "Of course, it's a different time of day, and we won't be driving into it. That would be so indelicate, don't you think?"

Audra saw Zoey swallow, hard. Perfect. Now the girl knew she was serious. But did she know how serious?

Deadly.

Audra threw open her door and jumped out of the car, doing a little dance and waving her arms in the air. She hadn't felt this good in several hours and she wanted to really let go. But she had to get back to her guest.

Audra took several steps toward the car and pulled her keys out of her pocket. She dangled them in front of Zoey tauntingly. Zoey looked a little freaked out, which was no surprise. "What are you going to do now?" Audra asked with a laugh.

Audra knew people at Stafford thought she was a nut, but so what? Genius was often mistaken for insanity. Other people were just too stupid to understand. Including Zoey.

Audra sneered at her academic rival, who was still gripping the seat of the Audi TT. She had never believed the rumors about Zoey burning down her old school — Zoey wasn't clever enough.

"Think you're so smart?" Audra asked, still dangling the keys. "How are you going to get home without these?" She laughed and raced to the other side of the bridge, her entire body tingling with exhilaration. Why had she waited so long to do this? It was so long overdue, so perfectly clear. . . .

Audra felt the cold air course through her lungs as she leaned out over the edge of the bridge. She felt so alive! She hung her head over the drop and stared into the abyss where the rocky river tumbled below, framed by yellow- and orange-leaved trees.

It was going to be a beautiful fall.

Chapter Thirty-nine

Zoey stared at Audra as she spun crazily in circles, waving her arms in the air and dangling the keys, taunting her. She'd known the girl was loony, but she had never seen her act this outright psychotic. It was a miracle her brother had survived all that time he'd spent with her — assuming he actually *had* survived.

As Audra walked back toward the car with her keys jingling, Zoey reached down to unbuckle her seat belt. But the locking mechanism seemed to be jammed — she couldn't get free! As Audra closed in, Zoey rammed down harder and harder on the orange plate. She felt a cold, fearful panic rush over her.

"You seem agitated," Audra said in a sickeningly calm voice as she leaned in through the open driver's-side window.

Finally the buckle released and the strap slackened. Zoey threw the strap over her shoulder and shook herself free. A moment later she was standing outside the car, truly relieved to be free of at least one of Audra's webs.

Zoey watched as Audra backed slowly up to the edge of the bridge and sat down on the metal rail. *You can have your keys*, Zoey thought. *All I need is a ride.*

Pulling her cell phone out of her bag, she flipped it open.

"No service!" Audra said in singsong.

Zoey opened the phone to make sure. No service.

"I thought of everything. I always do." Audra kicked one leg over the edge and let it dangle.

Zoey walked toward the road, trying to get a couple of bars. Nothing. Nada. Not even the clock was working.

"Crap!" Zoey yelled, shoving the phone into her pocket. She had no choice but to try to get the keys from the lunatic who'd brought her out here. She had not forgotten for a second that her brother was somewhere else, needing her.

What was I thinking getting into the car with her? Zoey wondered as she planned her approach. She'd been warning her brother about doing just that for weeks. It was so ironic that she had done it for him. And where did it get her? Stranded on a bridge, playing cat and mouse with the school whacko by the lake her mother had died in. Some savior she was. For all she knew, Tom was back at school banging his head into a locker — or worse.

Zoey winced. She had to get back to school to find her brother.

Zoey spoke as calmly as she could. "Audra, I think Tom's in serious trouble. I need to get to him before he does something stupid."

Audra glared at her. "He's in trouble all right. But for someone who gets such good grades, you are a complete idiot." She rolled her eyes, as if it were obvious to everyone except Zoey. "*You're* the one who needs help now," she said tauntingly.

Huh? Zoey had no idea what she meant.

"Don't you get it, Zoey? Tom's problem is

you. He's been complaining about you for weeks, telling me how he wishes you'd just disappear. Don't you know? Your brother hates you!"

Zoey stumbled back a little, feeling like she'd been kicked in the chest. Audra's words rang far too true. Her brother probably did hate her — he certainly acted like it.

It doesn't matter, Zoey told herself. *I'm not giving up on him.* She looked down at the water far below. She couldn't give up — not now. "I still need to get to him," Zoey said, speaking a little more softly.

Audra laughed maniacally, swung her leg back over the guardrail, and stepped closer.

Good. The keys still dangled from the tip of her finger.

"You think you can beat me? You can't. I'm the smartest student Stafford has ever seen . . . or ever will see." Audra kept coming closer to Zoey, a crazy look in her eye. Zoey backed up, luring her away from one side of the bridge. She didn't notice they were getting ever closer to the other side until she backed into it.

Whoa. Zoey circled her arms to regain her

balance. She looked over her shoulder. It was a l-o-n-g way down.

"Forget about school," Zoey said calmly. She had to play it cool. The last thing she wanted was an even-more-over-the-edge Audra. "It really doesn't matter to me," Zoey assured her. "I'm not trying to take anything away from you."

"You think you can fool me. You and Kelly think you rule the world, rule Tom Ramirez," Audra sneered. "Only you don't. He's mine. Mine!" Audra shook as fury overtook her. Her keys jangled wildly, but her eyes were even wilder.

Zoey quickly stepped away from the edge, but Audra closed in faster and blocked her way. "Where you going, smarty-pants?" Audra asked, leering.

Zoey took a breath. As freaky as this whole scene was, she had to stay calm. "Nowhere," she said, backing up again. "But just so we're clear, my brother isn't yours. Or mine. Or Kelly's. He's a *person*. Nobody can possess him."

"*I* can!" Audra screamed. "I can and I will! Tom confides in me. He tells me everything, and

I listen. I understand. He loves me, not you, and *not* Kelly Reeves!"

Audra dropped her hands to her sides, totally dejected, as if she knew her words were not even remotely true. But then her expression changed to one of resolve. "I just have to prove that I'll do anything for him. I have to help him get free of everything, of everyone. Of you."

Zoey felt a tingle run down her spine. That was a threat.

"You can't keep Tom away from me!" Audra screamed. "Nobody can!"

Before Zoey knew what was happening, Audra came at her in one giant lunge. Zoey dodged at the last second, and watched in shock as Audra hit the guardrail with such force that she flipped over it. One arm flew free but the hand still clutching the keys grasped for a hold.

"No!" Zoey screamed. It happened in an instant. Zoey raced to the edge as fast as she could, reaching out to grab Audra and pull her back up. Her fingers brushed the sleeve of Audra's jacket, but before she could get a grasp, Audra's arm slipped and she fell. Audra's sharp, dry laugh echoed as she hurtled through the air toward the water and rocks below.

Zoey sank to her knees as she watched Audra plummet. When she hit the water, there was a loud *crack*, and Audra was thrown to the side from the impact. A moment later her lifeless body disappeared under the white, frothing water.

The drama continues in book four, *Life or Death*. Here's a sneak peek.

This is it. Alison closed her eyes and took a deep breath to calm her racing heart. The door was finally open, room 128 was right in front of her, and she could finally see Chad. Only one thing still stood in her way.

Kelly. Alison's best-friend-turned-nemesis had struck a pose, right in the middle of the doorway. So typical. Kelly was the last to arrive and the first in line.

Alison could not help but notice that her cousin was wearing a different skirt than the one she'd had on at school, and new Anna Sui boots. Freshly applied eye shadow shimmered on her lids as she gave Alison's rumpled outfit a once-over and made a face.

"Gross," Kelly said, eyeing the bloodstain on Alison's shirt. "You're a mess, Al. I can't believe Grandmother Diamond lets you go out like that."

Alison glared back. She did not care that she had Chad's dried blood on her. It was a badge of honor, because she had been there with him. *She* had never left him. *She* had stayed by his side, or as close as she could get, since this nightmare had started.

"So sorry," Alison hissed sarcastically. "I didn't have time to shower and change. I thought Chad might need me."

"Why would he need *you*?" Kelly asked, giving her a "you're so pathetic" look. "He has *me.*"

Alison balled her hands into fists, shoved them in her pockets, and willed herself to stay calm. She could not let Kelly get to her. Not here. Not now. She was here for Chad. Chad was all that mattered.

Taking a deep breath, Alison followed Kelly into Chad's room. What she saw made her gasp.

Chad was lying deathly still on the hospital bed surrounded by beeping and pinging machines. He had wires taped to his chest and tubes coming out of his arms, attached to his finger, and poking out of his gown. He looked like a marionette waiting for someone to pull his strings. His face was almost peaceful, and Alison saw his eyelids flutter — like he was dreaming and about to wake up. She willed his big brown eyes to open, to smile into hers. They didn't.

Unable to look away, Alison watched as Chad's chest rose and fell slowly. He was breathing on his own. That was something. But he looked incredibly pale against the crisp white sheets, and as fragile as the thin blue gown they had dressed him in.

Tearing her eyes away from Chad, Alison looked to see Kelly's reaction. The girl could not hide her distaste. Her nose was wrinkled as she gingerly picked her way past the IV and stationed herself in the only chair in the room — right next to Chad's bedside. Tom stood in one corner, biting his lip. Alison picked a spot in the other corner. She stood still, waiting for the curly-haired boy on the bed —*her* boy — to awake. The last words he had spoken before he'd collapsed echoed in her head. *I still love you.* Her heart ached at the thought, and she wished once more that she'd gotten the chance to tell him that she still loved him, too. She hoped more than anything that she wasn't too late.